MOONSHINER'S SON

CAROLYN REEDER

MOONSHINER'S SON

ALADDIN PAPERBACKS
New York London Toronto Sydney Singapore

First Aladdin Paperbacks edition March 2003
Originally published in 1993 by Macmillan Publishing Company
Text copyright © 1993 by Carolyn Reeder

ALADDIN PAPERBACKS
An imprint of Simon & Schuster
Children's Publishing Division
1230 Avenue of the Americas
New York, NY 10020

Printed in the United States of America
6 8 10 9 7

The Library of Congress has cataloged the hardcover edition as follows:
Reeder, Carolyn.
Moonshiner's son / Carolyn Reeder.—1st ed.
p. cm.
Summary: As he works with his father making moonshine in the remote hills of Virginia during Prohibition, twelve-year-old Tom learns about hard work and independent thinking.
ISBN 0-02-775805-2
[1. Fathers and sons—Fiction. 2. Mountain life—Virginia—Fiction.
3. Prohibition—Fiction.] I. Title.
PZ7.R25416Mo 1993
[Fic]—dc20 92-39570
ISBN 0-689-85550-8 (Aladdin pbk.)
0512 OFF

For my daughter, Linda

MOONSHINER'S SON

1

Tom lay flat on his stomach in the laurel thicket. He blew at the gnats that had been pestering him all day and tried to ignore the high-pitched hum of the sweat bee hovering around his ear. A towhee scratched in the leaves a few yards away, chirping its "Sweet bird-eeee!" call at regular intervals. The only other sound was the bubbling and spitting of the barrels of mash fermenting beside the creek, screened by the branches of a fallen tree.

"If they're comin', they'd better come soon," Tom muttered. He didn't want to spend a third day like this, and Pa couldn't relish another night hunkered down, waiting to see if whoever had shortened his last run of whiskey by pouring salt into one of the mash barrels was going to do it again.

Who could it have been? Tom went over the possibilities in his mind for the hundredth time. A revenuer wouldn't have advertised his presence by tampering with the mash—he'd have kept watch and caught the moonshiner and then destroyed the still. Tom frowned. What kind of man poured salt into a mash barrel, anyway? An angry man would have smashed it open. And a coward—or Eddie Jarvis, who coveted Pa's customers—would have told the sheriff where to find the still and let the law do his dirty work.

For a moment Tom wondered if someone could have done it as a joke, but he quickly discarded that idea. Messing around with a man's still was no joking matter. It wasn't something you did if you wanted to keep on living.

Suddenly a squirrel's scolding chatter made Tom's heartbeat quicken. Listening now, he heard splashing. Somebody was coming up the creek, and not even trying to be quiet about it!

Tom blinked in astonishment as a piebald horse came into view, making its way up the gravelly creek bed. Peering through the laurel growing near the bank, Tom could see the rider's high black boots. He held his breath, hoping the horse would pass him, but it stopped and the rider dismounted.

Tom's mouth dropped open. It was a girl! And she was wearing fancy riding pants like the ones in that mail-order catalog he'd seen at the Rigsbys' house. Tom watched, scarcely breathing, while the girl unbuckled the flap of her saddlebag and lifted something out. Tom raised his head a little. It looked like—it *was!* It was a five-pound sack of salt.

Ignoring the branches that scraped along his spine, Tom scuttled backward till he could stand up. Then he forced his way forward through the almost impenetrable greenery until he stood on the low creek bank, looking down at the girl.

She let the salt fall to the ground and stood facing him, an opened penknife in her hand. Tom grinned. You'd never see a knife like that at Ol' Man Barnes's store down in the settlement, he thought, looking at its tiny blade.

"Don't you come any closer," the girl warned. Her dark hair was pulled back into a thick braid, and her wide brown eyes were steady.

Suddenly conscious of his rumpled shirt and overalls and his unruly mop of sandy hair, Tom slid down the sloping bank and stood on the damp ground, opposite the girl. "You don't belong here," he said, trying to sound authoritative, like Pa. "Put away your pretty li'l knife an' go on back to where you come from."

Slowly the girl lowered her arm, but she made no move to leave. The horse, its nostrils quivering, was trying to force its way through the branches of the fallen tree that hid the mash barrels, and Tom quickly took the reins and turned the animal away. "Now git on, an' git out of here," he told the girl.

"I'll leave when I've done what I came to do, and not before," she said, her chin lifted defiantly.

In one swift movement, Tom leaned over and scooped up the sack of salt.

"Give me that. It's mine!" the girl demanded.

Tom shook his head. "I'm gonna"—he searched for the word—"*confiscate* it. Now git!"

The girl's eyes blazed with anger, and she didn't move.

Tom shrugged and tossed the sack into the shallow creek. "Folks hereabouts don't take kindly to anybody messin' 'round near their stills," he said sternly, turning back to the girl.

"Stills are illegal! Haven't you heard of Prohibition?"

Tom scowled. He'd heard of Prohibition, all right. How he hated the 1919 law that sent even more law officers into the hills to look for stills to destroy and moonshiners to arrest. Until two years ago, federal revenue agents had searched out moonshiners because they paid no taxes on the whiskey they made in secret. But now the revenuers came to enforce the new law against making or selling alcoholic drinks anywhere in the United States.

"I've heard of Pro'bition, all right," Tom said, "but maybe you ain't never heard of trespassin'. Trespassin's illegal, too," he said, "an' you're on my pa's land." He saw a flicker of concern cross the girl's face and pressed his advantage. "What would your people say if they knew you was trespassin'? An' if they found out you was foolin' 'round somebody's still?"

"They aren't going to find out," she said, but she didn't sound so confident now. She turned away from Tom and mounted her horse. "Anyway," she said, looking over her shoulder, "running a still is a lot worse than trespassing." With that, she tossed her head and rode downstream without looking back.

Tom gave the girl a long head start before he set off for home, glad he didn't have to lie hidden in the laurel thicket any longer. He splashed down the creek until it flowed across a narrow path, where he turned uphill. He was panting by the time the path intersected a wider trail that led further up the mountain.

As he neared the cabin and saw his father working in the corn patch on the hillside, Tom called, "Pa! Hey, Pa! I found out who spoilt our mash!"

The burly man leaned on his hoe and said with mock ferocity, "I hope you don't expect me to believe it was a brown-eyed li'l gal on a piebald horse."

"How—how did you know?" Tom stammered.

Pa threw back his head and laughed. "Set yourself down under that there tree, an' I'll tell you."

Surprised to find Pa in such good humor, Tom followed him to the shade of the white oak that towered over their cabin. Pa leaned back against its trunk, and Tom sat cross-legged, facing him.

"Wal," Pa began, "I thought I'd walk on down to the store to buy a pound of coffee an' hear the news, an' while I was there, this li'l gal rode up, wearin' some of them pants that make 'em look like their hips has slid halfway to their knees. She marched right into the store and asked for a sack of salt. A *bag* of salt, she called it.

"After Ol' Man Barnes got it for her, he said she was more 'n welcome to git a drink from the pump over by his house, since she must be mighty thirsty. An' when she allowed as how she didn't know what he meant, he said, 'If your ma's used up all that salt you bought here last week, I'd think you'd have a powerful thirst.' "

Tom grinned appreciatively. Pa sure knew how to tell a tale.

"Then she told him that there salt weren't for her ma, so I ask, real surprised like, 'You mean to say it's for your *pa?*' But she shakes her head an' says she's buyin' it for herself, an' out she goes. Last I seen her, she was ridin' up the trail."

Remembering how the girl had stood up to him, Tom asked, "What's a girl like her doin' 'round here, anyway?"

"Her pa's the preacher settin' up that mission down at the ol' Ollie Gentry place. He's the one that's been ridin' through Ox Gore Holler talkin' about the evils of drink," Pa said contemptuously.

Tom scowled. Weeks ago, he'd listened while Ol' Man Barnes had read the newspaper story telling how some city church was planning to set up a mission here in the hills. The storekeeper had repeated the last sentence twice, and Tom hadn't forgotten it: "It is hoped that the mission will provide a civilizing influence on the lawless and un-lettered people in this wild area of the Virginia Blue Ridge."

Pa's voice brought Tom back to the present. "That preacher hired men from Buckton to come out an' fix up the house, since nobody 'round here would work for him. Eddie Jarvis tried to run them workmen off, but the preacher was there with 'em, an' he stood right up to Eddie—said he was wearin' the armor of the Lord an' he wasn't scared of no shotgun." Pa paused to let that sink in and then mused, "That man's either powerful brave, or else he's a fool."

Tom thought he must be a fool if he couldn't see he wasn't welcome here. Unless he just plain didn't care.

"What I can't figger out," Pa said, changing the subject, "is how that slip of a gal happened on my still."

"She rode up the creek," Tom said.

Pa's good humor vanished. "Dadburn it, boy! Did you empty the slop from the still into the creek even though I told you to carry it to the hogs?"

"I carried most of it to the hogs, but—"

"But some of it you dumped in the creek," Pa broke in angrily. "Trust you to work by yourself, an' next thing I know somebody finds their way to my still!"

Tom didn't see the connection, but he wasn't about to ask. When Pa was mad, the best thing to do was keep quiet and stay out of his way.

"Don't you know you're as good as advertisin' the location of your still if you dump your slop in the creek when you clean it out?"

Tom shook his head, not daring to speak.

"Dadburn revenuer's horse'll give you away every time. Most of 'em turn up their noses an' won't drink water with the smell of mash in it, but if you git one that likes it, he'll follow the stream right up to your still. Either way, you're in trouble. It's a good thing that piebald horse didn't have no revenuer on his back."

Tom had thought feeding the slop to the hogs was just a way to keep them from going completely wild while they roamed along the mountainside, eating acorns and chestnuts. A way to keep them used to coming to your call so they'd be easier to round up at butchering time in the fall. "I'm sorry, Pa," he said. "I didn't know it was important."

Before Tom realized what was happening, Pa grabbed the front of his shirt and pulled him so close that they were almost nose to nose. "Listen here, boy," Pa said. "When I tell you to do somethin', you better figure it's important. An' you better do it even if you don't understand why. You hear me?" Pa's voice was deadly quiet, and his pale blue eyes were cold.

"I hear!" Tom choked out. "I hear you, Pa."

"Then make sure you remember," Pa said harshly, releasing him. Miserable, Tom watched his father walk back to the corn patch. Disobeying out of laziness was bad enough, Tom realized, but deliberately not doing what he was told was even worse. When Pa gave orders, he wanted them followed—and he usually found out when they weren't.

Tom went into the cabin and took his whittling knife and a small block of maple from the mantel. Already the rough figure of a chipmunk was emerging from the wood. "I could of had this finished by now if Pa hadn't made me leave it home when I was on watch at the still," Tom muttered. But then he thought of what could have happened if he'd been concentrating on his carving when the girl on the horse came up the creek. She might have thrown the salt into one of Pa's mash barrels before he'd been able to stop her! He didn't even want to think about what Pa would have said if that had happened.

2

Tom watched Ol' Man Barnes pour the lantern fuel into his can and stick a potato on the spout so that none of the liquid would splash out as he walked home. While the storekeeper wrote the price in his ledger book, Tom studied the letters on the man's large container: K-e-r-o-s-e-n-e spells *coal oil*, he rehearsed silently.

It bothered Tom that he was twelve years old and couldn't read. But at least he wasn't "unlettered." Ma had taught him to make his letters before she'd taken his two little sisters and gone off, leaving a note that said, "This is no life for a woman." Ever since then, it had been just him and Pa, and Pa wouldn't teach him to read. He said a moonshiner didn't need book learning.

Ol' Man Barnes interrupted Tom's thoughts. "Tell your pa a stranger was hangin' 'round here yesterday. Never really said where he come from, just that he spent a lot of time in the hills."

"You'd think a revenuer would have him some kind of a story," Tom mused, "but like Pa says, you can't be too careful." As he left the store, Tom glanced around, hoping to see his friends Lonny and Harry, but no one was in sight. Disappointed, he set off for home to tell Pa what Ol' Man Barnes had said.

Tom wasn't surprised at the storekeeper's news. Yesterday afternoon he'd heard someone fire two widely spaced shots—the signal that a stranger was in the area—and he'd relayed the warning up the hollow with Pa's rifle. That was why he'd filled both the lamps this morning, emptying the fuel can so he'd have an excuse to walk down to the little settlement at Nathan's Mill and see what was going on. After what he'd learned, he knew that this afternoon he'd have the tiresome duty of keeping watch while Pa finished setting up the still under the rocky overhang he'd chosen for the new location.

Strangers came into Bad Camp Hollow for only two reasons: to buy moonshine, or to catch the men who made it. If this stranger wanted to buy moonshine, he could buy Pa's whiskey at Ol' Man Barnes's store, provided he knew what to say when he asked for it. If he was a revenuer—well, Pa was always careful, but it helped to know when your enemy was around.

Tom thought of the girl he'd met two days before. Pitching his voice high, he mimicked her, "Stills are il-le-gal." If she thought stills were so bad, she should have stayed wherever it was she'd come from. Shifting the can of lantern fuel to his other hand, Tom began the steepest part of his climb up the mountain. Suddenly, a piercing scream brought him to a halt and made the hairs on his arms stand on end. When he heard the frightened neighing of a horse, he left his can and ran back down the trail. He rounded the bend and saw the piebald horse rearing and the girl clinging to its mane. And beneath the horse's hooves was what was left of the biggest rattlesnake Tom had ever seen. His stomach turned at the thought of how recently he'd passed that very spot, his mind a mile away.

Tearing his eyes from the mangled snake, Tom grabbed the reins, pulled the horse around, and led it a short distance downhill. It pranced about, flanks heaving, but Tom's firm hand on the reins kept it from rearing.

"I'll lead him past that snake so he don't spook again an' throw you," Tom said, looking up at the girl.

"I can manage my own horse, thank you very much," she said, yanking the reins out of his hand.

Tom saw that her face was pale and her eyes were still dark with fear. Or was it anger? Rebuffed, he turned away, and she maneuvered the horse so that it was facing uphill again.

"What are you *doing?*" she asked when Tom bent over the trampled snake.

He wiped off the blade of his knife and snapped it shut. "Don't you want these?" he asked, holding up the snake's rattles. "Listen," he said, shaking them.

At that, the horse snorted and tossed its head, but the girl handled it skillfully. "You can have them," she said with distaste.

Pleased, Tom put the rattles in his pocket and started up the hill. But before he came to his can of lantern fuel, the girl called to him.

"Hey! Hey, you!"

Tom hesitated, and she called again, louder this time. "Hey, you!" And then after a brief pause, "Can you please come back here for a minute?"

Tom retraced his steps. "Thought you could manage your own horse," he said when he saw it shying and refusing to pass the mangled snake.

"I can! But I need you to move that snake."

Tom took the reins again, and raising the horse's head slightly, he led the animal several yards beyond the snake. Then he stepped aside to let the girl ride past. But to his surprise she swung down from the saddle and stood facing him.

"My name's Amy," she said. "Amy Taylor."

"Mine's Tom Higgins."

Amy eyed his can suspiciously. "What's in there?" she demanded.

"What do you think?" Tom asked, grinning. Quick as a flash, Amy grabbed for the can, and he cried, "Look out! You're gonna spill my coal oil."

"Coal oil? I thought it was liquor. My father says Bad Camp Hollow just flows with liquor." Amy wrinkled up her nose and said, "That smells like kerosene to me."

"Wal, it's coal oil: k-e-r-o-s-e-n-e," said Tom. "Don't they learn you nothin' about respectin' other folks' property where you're from? First you come on my pa's land an' ruin his mash, an' now you try to spill my coal oil."

"I'm sorry about your, um, coal oil," she said, "but I'm glad I ruined your father's—what did you call it?"

"Mash."

"I don't care if it was on his own land. I'll do anything I can to work against the evils of drink."

"You're gonna git yourself in trouble if you keep messin' 'round people's stills," Tom warned.

Amy tossed her head and said, "When my father's through here, there won't be a still left. You just wait and see."

"He's fixin' to git hisself killed."

"Killed? Nobody'd kill a minister of the gospel, would they?"

Tom snorted. "Long as he sticks to preachin' the gospel, they won't. That's his business, right?"

"Yes, but—"

"Long as he minds his own business he'll be safe enough." Tom started up the trail again, and when Amy called after him, he ignored her. How dare she and her father come here and try to tell him and Pa what to do? When he heard the ring of hooves striking rocks on the rough path and the scrabble of Amy's boots close behind him, he wheeled around and faced her.

"Stop follerin' me!"

"I'm not following you. This is the way I'm going."

"Go on then," Tom said, standing aside.

Amy bit her lip. "Look, I didn't mean to make you mad. Can't we start all over? Hi, my name's Amy Taylor."

Tom grinned in spite of himself. "I'm Tom Higgins. What do you call him?" He gestured toward the horse.

"He's Agamemnon."

"Aga—what?"

"Agamemnon. My father named both our horses after kings in a famous book about the ancient Greeks. He has a big gray horse named Odysseus."

Agamemnon and Odysseus? "Never heard of givin' innocent critters names like those," Tom said doubtfully.

"As long as we're talking about names, where did anybody dream up one like Bad Camp Hollow?" Amy asked.

"It used to be Higgins Holler, 'cause mostly Higginses lived 'round here back then. That's Higgins Run down there," he said, nodding toward the stream some distance below the path, "an' this is Higgins Mountain. Anyways, a while back, two strangers came an' set up their tent an' told folks they was studyin' the plants. Walked all through the woods.

"Nobody knew for sure they wasn't revenuers, so some of the men kind of encouraged 'em to leave by settin' a few fires ahead of 'em an' then, after they started back, a few more on either side of where they was. Them fellers hightailed it back to their tent an' packed up, an' when they went through the settlement, they told the miller they'd decided this was a bad place to camp. Ever since then, it's been Bad Camp Holler."

"Those men could have caused a terrible forest fire!" Amy said indignantly.

Tom looked at her with amusement. "It just made a lot of smoke and burned off some brush."

"Do people still set fires like that?"

"You won't have to worry none, long as you an' Agamemnon—an' your pa—stay on the path."

Tom heard Amy draw a quick breath. "Are you threatening me, Tom Higgins?" she asked.

"I'm warnin' you," he said seriously.

"Well, you don't scare me, and *nobody's* going to scare my father," Amy said. And with one smooth motion she was back in the saddle, urging Agamemnon up the trail.

Tom stood looking after them, wondering what would happen if Amy's folks found out what she was up to when she went out riding.

3

Tom figured he'd been sitting beside the creek facing downstream for a good two hours, and the most dangerous thing he'd seen was a squirrel. Even if there had been a stranger down at the store yesterday, that was a long way from here. And just because Amy had stumbled onto Pa's still didn't mean she'd come looking to find where they'd moved it to, did it?

Tom tried to forget that it was his fault that Amy—or rather, Agamemnon—had found Pa's still. But he knew he had only himself to blame for the fact that he was sitting there, keeping watch while Pa worked. Tom sighed, wishing he could see how Pa would divert water from the stream to the sheltered spot where he'd set up the still. How exactly would he use that length of metal pipe he'd brought with him?

Shifting to a more comfortable position, Tom decided that being lookout was worse than anything else Pa made him do. Carrying rocks and mixing mud for mortar while Pa built the furnace around the still pot yesterday had been hard work, but at least it hadn't been dull.

Tom reached into his pocket and pulled out the chipmunk he'd been whittling. Already he could tell it would be the best carving he'd ever done. When it was finished, he'd keep it on the mantel, where he could admire it. As he held the perky little wooden animal, Tom's hands almost tingled with longing to work on it, but he slipped it back into his pocket. Pa had said to keep watch, and this time he was going to do as he'd been told.

But it was so tiresome. Sighing, Tom broke off a twig from the bush behind him and tossed its leaves into the current, one at a time, following them with his eyes until they were out of sight. He half wished he'd hear someone coming so he could run and warn Pa. They would disappear into the forest and silently make their way back to the cabin, and then Pa would say, I'm proud of you, boy. You done good.

"Woolgatherin' again!"

Tom gave a start and scrambled to his feet. "I was keepin' watch, Pa! Honest!"

Pa glared at Tom and said, "Coulda fooled me."

As he followed Pa downstream, Tom thanked his lucky stars that the chipmunk carving had been safely in his pocket.

After supper Tom and Pa went out on the porch to shell corn from last year's harvest. Tom fed the ears into the hopper of the corn sheller, and Pa turned the crank on the side of the boxy wooden machine. Bare cobs flew from a chute in front, and a steady stream of yellow kernels flowed from an opening at the bottom and dropped into a bucket. As soon as the bucket was full, Tom replaced it with another and poured the kernels into a sack.

When a man on a huge gray horse rode up to the gate, Tom was ready for an excuse to stop the noisy, dusty work. He watched the man dismount, throw his reins over the gatepost, and stride toward the porch.

"I understand you're planning to kill me, Higgins," the man said, leaning toward Pa, his chin out-thrust. Tom could almost feel his anger.

"Pa," he said in a tight voice, "I think this here's Mr. Taylor, from down at that mission."

Pa straightened up and looked the man over, from the cap on his wavy brown hair down to his shiny riding boots. Then he spit a stream of tobacco juice just past him. "You heard that, did you?" he said finally.

The preacher gave a quick nod.

"An' you're standin' here now?" Pa asked, a gleam of amusement in his eye.

The preacher nodded again.

"Wal," Pa drawled, "then it must not of been true, 'cause if I ever plan to kill a man, he won't live to come an' ask me about it." Turning to Tom, he said, "Boy, git this man a drink."

The preacher took a step back and said, "I've dedicated my life to ridding the Virginia Blue Ridge of the evils of drink, and—"

Pa let his jaw drop. "Why, 'round here, offerin' a neighbor a drink of water after a long, hot ride is considered the decent thing to do."

Tom held out a gourd of water dipped from the bucket by the door and asked, "Don't you want this?" The preacher took the gourd from him and held it awkwardly, and Tom said, "I'll go water Odysseus for you now. Is he named for the king in that Greek book?"

Looking surprised, the preacher nodded.

"That's a right famous story," Tom said, hiding a grin as he headed toward the spring.

When Tom came back to the porch, the preacher was telling Pa how he'd felt called to leave his church in Richmond and come into the Virginia mountains to convince the people to give up making and drinking liquor. "Remember what the Bible tells us: 'Wine is a mocker, strong drink is raging, and whosoever is deceived thereby is not wise,' " he said with finality. Pointing to the rows of corn growing on the hillside opposite the cabin, he said, "For a crop that large to be turned into liquor instead of corn-meal is an abomination in the eyes of the Lord."

"Except what I use for animal feed, that whole crop's gonna end up as cornmeal," Pa said honestly.

Preacher Taylor looked dubious, and Tom realized the man didn't know that cornmeal was the main ingredient used in making whiskey. The preacher didn't have any idea how much corn it took to supply a still, either. Their corncrib would be empty long before harvest time, and then Pa would switch to making fruit brandy.

"What's your yield per acre?" Preacher Taylor asked.

"Don't rightly know how many gallon I get."

The preacher's face flushed and he seemed to control his anger with difficulty, but all he said was, "I can see I have my work cut out for me here." After an awkward pause, he said stiffly, "It's nearly dark, so I'll be on my way."

"You'll need this," Pa said, lighting a lantern and hand-ing it to the preacher. "It'll be black as the inside of your cap before you're home tonight."

Preacher Taylor's expression changed to one of appre-ciation as he reached for the lantern. "I'll send this back with my daughter sometime tomorrow."

"The boy can walk down to your place for it in the mornin'," Pa said.

That was fine with Tom. Any errand was better than spending hour after weary hour as Pa's lookout at the still.

The preacher quickly agreed. "After all, when we get a school built, he'll be walking down there every morning."

Pa didn't answer, and Tom stared at the ground. He

knew the only schooling he'd ever have would be learning the craft of making whiskey.

Mounting Odysseus, the preacher said, "I'd heard illiteracy was rampant in these hills, but this boy knows the Greek myths, and my daughter says he can spell, too. Well, there's still a lot for him to learn. The Bible says, 'Give instruction to a wise man and he will be yet wiser,' and I guess that goes for boys, too."

As the bobbing circle of lantern light disappeared into the dusk, Pa said, "Come on back to the porch an' tell me that Greek story you like so well before we turn in."

"Amy—that's the preacher's girl—told me their horses was named for the Greek kings in some book. I was just pretendin' I knew the story," Tom admitted.

After a moment Pa challenged, "An' how'd you just pretend you could spell?"

"I learned to spell *coal oil* down at the store. An' when Amy thought I had whiskey in my can, I told her it was nothin' but coal oil: k-e-r-o-s-e-n-e. I guess I was showin' off."

Pa was silent for a moment, and then he said harshly, "When they get that school built down at the mission, you're goin' to it, you hear?"

Tom's heart leaped. "I hear," he said, "but how come you changed your mind?"

" 'Cause what you spelled was *kerosene*, an' I don't want no son of mine makin' a fool of hisself like that again."

Tom felt as though he'd been punched in the belly. "But—"

"That's what the flatlanders call coal oil," Pa said, spitting out *flatlanders* with withering contempt.

Tom stared into the darkness, his excitement about going to school forgotten.

4

The next morning, Tom tucked in his shirttail and slicked down his hair with water before he started off to get the lantern. This was his chance to satisfy his curiosity about the mission and keep an eye out for the mysterious stranger at the same time.

Leaving the trail to the settlement, Tom turned onto the steep path that led to the bottomland along Jenkins Branch. As he splashed across the shallow creek that Amy and Agamemnon had followed to Pa's still, Tom vowed that somehow he would prove that he could be trusted. He'd make Pa proud of him yet.

At last Tom reached Jenkins Branch and crossed on the footlog. He was walking along the old wagon road that paralleled the stream when his eye fell on a bootprint in the mud near the edge. A man even bigger than Pa had walked here, and not long ago, either. It must have been the mysterious stranger the storekeeper had warned him about—the tread of that boot sole wasn't one Tom recognized.

He continued along the narrow road, keeping his eyes peeled for more signs of the stranger. But he saw only horseshoe prints and the narrow ruts left by wagon wheels. "Probably from the Taylors movin' in their household goods," he mused aloud.

When Tom reached the mission, he stopped and stared. He hardly recognized the old Gentry place. The board-and-batten siding of the weather-beaten house had been repaired and given a coat of whitewash, the chestnut-shake roof had been replaced with shiny tin, and the door was painted red.

While Tom was admiring the mission house, Amy came out, wearing a blue dress and carrying the lantern. As she walked across the clearing, she looked back and waved, and Tom saw a woman standing in the doorway. She wasn't a pretty woman, but Tom liked the way she looked—like—well, like a mother.

As Amy walked toward him, Tom noticed that for once she didn't seem angry. Little tendrils of hair had escaped from her thick braid and curled around her face, giving it a softer look. Stepping into the clearing, Tom blurted out, "Didn't your pa tell you I was comin' for that there lantern?"

"Yes, but I needed an excuse to get away for a while. I'll just walk along with you, since you're here," she said, handing Tom the lantern. "I hate being around when Father's upset."

"What's he upset about?" Tom asked, not sure he wanted to walk with Amy.

"Somebody set fire to the lumber he'd bought for the mission's schoolhouse-chapel. Father smelled smoke late last night and went out there, but it was too late to save it. Come on, I'll show you."

Following Amy a short distance off the road to a pile of charred boards, Tom wondered if Eddie Jarvis had set the fire. When there was trouble, Eddie was usually behind it.

Amy wrinkled her nose at the acrid smell and asked, "Why would anybody do a thing like that?"

" 'Cause folks don't like the idea of havin' a mission in these hills," Tom said shortly as he turned back toward the road.

"Why not?" Amy asked in surprise, hurrying to catch up. "After all, the mission's being built to help them."

Tom struggled to control his anger. "Nobody 'round here asked for your help, did they?" he said bluntly. "You people come in here where nobody wants you, talkin' about how evil we are an' how you're gonna shut down our stills, an'—"

"It's the liquor that's evil, not the people," Amy objected. "There's a difference."

Tom said, "We don't try to tell your pa how to earn a livin', and he don't have no right to tell us how to, neither."

"Earn a living?" Amy echoed.

"Why else would a man make moonshine?" Tom asked in exasperation. "You think Pa likes carryin' them heavy sacks of cornmeal through the woods on his back? You think he likes settin' up all night feedin' the fire and makin' sure it don't get too hot? An' always worryin' about revenuers? 'Course he don't! But how else can he get money to pay his land tax? An' to buy me shoes for winter?" Tom stood glaring at Amy. " 'Course, you wouldn't understand that. You've even got shoes for summer, an' boots, too, an' fancy ridin' clothes, an' probably—"

"My riding clothes and everything else I have comes out of the missionary barrel," Amy said flatly.

"What's a missionary barrel?"

"It's a barrel full of things better-off people are tired of, so they send them to the missions for the needy."

Tom stared at Amy. "You take *charity?*"

Amy shrugged. "I guess you could call it that, but we look at it as part of Father's pay."

That made sense to Tom. Cash was in short supply in

the mountains, and neighbors often bartered for what they needed, or else they worked off the price.

"When Mother gets the mission's clothing bureau set up, you could get your shoes there. And a new shirt, too," Amy said pointedly.

"Pa and I don't take charity," Tom said stiffly, wishing he'd worn his other shirt. Even though it was tight across the shoulders, it didn't look so worn. He was tempted to tell Amy that Pa owned more land than anybody for miles around, land his ancestors had claimed when they came here long ago. Then she wouldn't think they were no-accounts.

"The clothing bureau won't be charity," Amy said. "You'll have to pay, but not nearly as much as you would for new things at Mr. Barnes's store."

Pa would be glad to hear about that clothing bureau, Tom thought as they approached the spot where the path up the mountain left the old wagon road. "This is where I turn off," he said, but to his surprise, instead of saying good-bye, Amy crossed the branch on the footlog and started uphill ahead of him.

"You'd best pace yourself," he said. "You'll wear yourself out before you're halfway up." But instead of slowing, Amy climbed even faster. At least she wouldn't have the breath to argue with him, Tom thought.

Much later, when the path met the main trail from the settlement, Tom said, "Our cabin's just up there a ways."

"Then I'd better turn back."

"You look like you could use a drink of water," Tom said when he saw how red and sweaty Amy was.

She hesitated. "Is your father going to be home?"

"What's the matter, you scared he'll say somethin'

about you messin' with his still?" Tom challenged.

"Of course not! And I am a little thirsty. Will it be all right with your mother if I come?"

Tom was surprised by the pang of sadness he felt at Amy's question. "Ma's been gone more 'n six years now," he said.

"Oh, Tom! I'm so sorry."

The warm sympathy in her voice seemed to loosen his tongue. "I wish I knew where she was, an' if I'll ever see her again," he said wistfully.

"She's in heaven, Tom, I just know she is," Amy said. "And you'll see her again in the sweet by-and-by." She began to hum the tune of the old hymn as she walked.

Tom couldn't bring himself to tell Amy the truth. Why hadn't he kept his mouth shut? He should have let her start back instead of giving her the chance to turn up her nose at their small, mud-chinked cabin with its sagging shake roof.

Tom opened the gate, and Amy headed straight for the rocking chair on the porch. As she sank into it, her eye fell on the open sack of corn Tom and Pa had shelled the night before. Her expression darkened and she said, "You're going to use that for corn liquor, aren't you?"

Before Tom could reply, a voice behind them said, "Moonshiners eat corn bread, same as anybody else, you know. Tom's takin' that there corn to Nathan's Mill this afternoon."

Amy was out of the chair and facing Pa in an instant, and Tom thought she looked a little frightened. "I—I just stopped to get a drink, Mr. Higgins," she said.

Pa looked down at her disapprovingly. "Drinkin's unseemly in a woman. An' you'll break your pa's heart, besides. Take my advice an' stay away from the eee-vils of likker." He looked at her sternly for a moment. Then he drank deeply from the water gourd and headed back to the corn patch.

Amy's face was pale, but her eyes glowed with anger. "He was making fun of me!"

"That's small punishment for all the trouble you caused," Tom said. "How'd you know salt would stop that mash from workin', anyhow?"

Amy looked puzzled. "I just wanted to make it taste bad so people wouldn't drink it," she said.

"You better not do nothin' like that again." If she ever stumbled onto Eddie Jarvis's still, she could be in real danger.

Defiantly, Amy said, "You can't tell me what to do, Tom Higgins."

"I ain't tellin' you nothin' different than your pa would if he knew what you'd been up to," Tom said, watching her carefully. Some of the color drained from her face, and Tom wasn't sure whether she was angry or afraid. "I bet he'd be a lot more upset to hear about what you done the other day than he was about losin' his lumber pile," he added.

"I'll make you a bargain," Amy said. "I'll stay away from your father's still, and you won't tell my father anything. Okay?"

Tom tried not to show his surprise that Amy took his veiled threat seriously. "You stay away from *all* stills," he said. "Find yourself some other way to work against the eee-vils of likker."

For a moment, Tom thought he had gone too far, but Amy grinned and said, "You sounded exactly like him!"

Then, serious again, she said, "So let's get this straight. I'll stay away from everybody's stills and you won't say a word to my father—or even hint to him—about what I did. All right?" When Tom nodded, wondering why she'd given in so easily, Amy stuck her hand out and looked at him expectantly. "We have to shake hands if it's going to be a binding agreement," she said impatiently. She grabbed his hand and shook it. Then, looking smug, she said, "I wouldn't have gone looking for stills, anyway, because this morning my father made me promise never to go off the trails."

"I wouldn't of told, either."

"I didn't really think you would," Amy said, her eyes meeting Tom's.

Flustered, he bent over to pick up the nearly empty bucket. "I—I'll get some more water so you can have your drink before you start home," he said. Amy was different from the mountain girls, and Tom wasn't quite sure what to make of her.

5

That noon, Tom sliced himself a hunk of leftover corn bread and spread a thick layer of butter on it. Pa might say drinking was unseemly in a woman, he thought, but that didn't stop him from supplying the Widow Brown with whiskey in return for butter and other vittles.

"You really want me to take that corn we shelled down

to the mill this afternoon?" he asked. "The sack ain't full yet."

"That's what I told that li'l gal, an' lyin' ain't one of my eee-vils," Pa said. "Besides, goin' to the mill will give you a excuse to check on things down at the settlement. I heard the signal again while you was gone."

"I almost forgot," Tom said. And then he told his father about the bootprint by Jenkins Branch.

"That ain't the kind of thing you forgit!" Pa said heatedly. "See that it don't happen again—ever, you hear?"

"I hear."

Pa sank back into his chair and mused, "Must of been that stranger Ol' Man Barnes told you about. But if he's a revenuer, he must be a beginner."

Pushing his chair back from the table, Tom said, "I'll see what I can find out down at the mill." He lugged the sack of shelled corn to the gate and went to whistle for Ol' Sal, the swaybacked mare grazing in the rocky pasture. A few minutes later, he was headed toward the settlement, riding atop the sack of corn.

At the mill, Tom tied Ol' Sal to the hitching rail between Cat Johnson's horse and Doc Mowbray's. He shouldered the sack of corn, trying not to stagger under its weight, and went into the mill. Sunlight shining through the window reflected from the dust floating in the air and made a wide golden beam. And at the end of the beam sat a man Tom had never seen before, a large man with reddish brown hair and a drooping mustache.

"Hey, Tom!" the miller called, interrupting his conversation with Cat Johnson and Doc Mowbray. And then he turned to the stranger. "This here's June Higgins's boy— you know, the one I was tellin' you about." The miller had to shout to make himself heard over the rumble of machinery.

The stranger stood up and walked over to Tom. "Pleased to meet you," he said, extending his hand. "My name's Paul Anderson. You can call me Andy."

Awkwardly, Tom shook the man's hand, wondering why anybody would be pleased to meet him.

"I'd like to talk to you, son," Andy said. "Let's go outside, away from all this noise."

Tom followed the man to the shade of a huge chestnut tree, his mind awhirl. Revenuers often hung around mills, hoping to catch moonshiners who took their sprouted grain to be ground, but the miller would never have given a revenuer Pa's name. He wouldn't have given Pa's name to a stranger looking for whiskey, either, because that was how some tricky revenuers operated. So why was this man interested in Pa?

Andy leaned against the tree trunk and opened his tobacco pouch, while Tom sat on the grass and watched him go through the ritual of filling and lighting his pipe. At last the sweet tobacco aroma drifted across the still air, and Andy spoke. "I understand you live a couple miles up the trail from here," he said.

Tom nodded. "The thing is, there's mad dogs loose on the mountain up there," he said, watching Andy closely. If the man was looking to buy moonshine, he'd reply, "Mad dogs don't scare me. It's mad men I worry about."

But Andy frowned and asked, "Are you sure? I hadn't heard about any rabies around here."

Shrugging, Tom said, "Could of been a pack of hounds bayin', I guess."

"Rabid dogs don't run in packs," Andy said, sounding relieved. Then he said, "So June Higgins is your mother."

Tom could hardly believe his ears. "He's my *father!*" he said indignantly.

Andy looked confused and embarrassed. "Sorry. Where I come from June's a woman's name."

"Well, 'round here it's short for Junior," Tom said.

Andy puffed on his pipe for a moment before he asked, "What's your father's full name, then?"

"Junior Higgins." What else could it be?

Andy's gray eyes were thoughtful, and after a moment he asked, "The younger man in the mill, is his full name Doctor Mowbray?"

"It's just Doc. His ma named him after ol' Doc Ennis, the doctor from town that cured her when she had typhoid."

Andy stared off into the distance, as though he were storing that piece of information away until he needed it. Then he looked directly at Tom. "I hear June Higgins is quite a storyteller."

Tom grinned. Pa was just about as well known for his stories as for his moonshine.

"I'd like to hear some of his stories," Andy continued. He leaned forward a little and said, "You see, I listen to people's stories and write them down. I'm going to put them in a book, and after each one, I'll say who told it and where they live."

Pa might be famous! "Cat Johnson there in the mill an' the Widow Brown tell 'em 'most as good as Pa, an' Jonah Simpson can tell a passable tale, too." Tom wanted to make sure Andy filled his book.

"I'll be boarding at Mrs. Brown's cabin, so maybe I can persuade her to tell me some of her stories."

"A drink of whiskey might loosen her tongue," Tom said, watching Andy closely.

Andy's eyes met Tom's. "Do you know where I can buy some whiskey?"

"I—I might be able to find out," Tom said, looking away. He was confused. Was Andy telling the truth, or was he a clever revenuer who won people's trust by listening to their stories?

"Let me know if you do," Andy said. After a pause he asked, "When would be a good time for me to meet your father?"

"How about two nights from now?" Tom suggested, not wanting to sound too eager.

"Two nights from now it is, then," Andy said as he got to his feet. "I'll holler when I come near."

Now Tom was more puzzled than ever. Hollering was the custom in the mountains, but outsiders didn't know that. Preacher Taylor sure didn't. Pa would have to figure it out, Tom thought as he watched Andy walk back to the mill.

Tom looked around when someone called his name, and he saw a sturdy dark-haired boy coming toward him, followed by a narrow-shouldered fellow whose arms looked too long for his body. It was Lonny Rigsby and his cousin, Harry Perkins.

"Wanna hunt crawdads with us?" Lonny asked.

"Sure," Tom said, standing up. He liked splashing through the creek and trying to catch the funny-looking little water creatures before they scurried under a rock— or pinched his fingers with their claws. "But I ain't got no pail."

"That don't matter," Lonny said cheerfully, " 'cause you probably won't find no crawdads."

Tom grinned as he fell into step with the other boys. "Probably not. An' if I do, I'll just give 'em to Harry."

"You hear about the fire Eddie Jarvis set last night?" Harry asked, ignoring the other boys' bantering.

So it *was* Eddie Jarvis. "You mean down at the mission?" Tom asked.

Harry nodded. "That preacher met up with him on the road an' commenced talkin' against whiskey. Quoted at him from the Bible."

"Made Eddie so mad he couldn't sleep," Lonny added, "so he got up an' went over there an' set fire to the preacher's lumber pile. Sort of as a warnin', like. Wish I could of seen it."

"Might make that preacher think twice before he starts tryin' to rid the holler of stills an' turn everybody away from drink," Harry added.

"It might," Tom said, but he didn't think for a minute that it would.

6

"I want you to take the Widow Brown some buttermilk," Pa said after breakfast the next day.

Buttermilk? Tom stared at him.

Pa grinned wickedly and said, "Go on 'round to the spring box an' git it."

Mystified, Tom went around the cabin to the small rectangular concrete cistern below the spring, where they cooled their perishables. Six two-quart jars of white liquid stood in the water that flowed through the spring box and nearly filled it. A smile spread across Tom's face as he unscrewed a lid and peered into one of the jars. Pa sure was clever. How had he ever thought of painting the insides of his jars white?

Tom put one in a sack, slung it over his shoulder, and started on his way, whistling. As he turned off the trail to the settlement and headed toward Jenkins Branch, he thought of Amy wearing herself out on the climb to the cabin the day before. She was one stubborn girl.

Tom had just crossed the footlog when he saw Amy riding toward him. "What's in that sack?" she demanded by way of greeting.

"Buttermilk for the Widow Brown," Tom lied, lifting out the jar for her to see.

Amy made a face. "We only drink sweet milk at our house." Swinging down from the saddle she said, "I'll walk along with you."

"But I'm goin' the other way."

She shrugged. "I wasn't going anywhere in particular."

As they started off together Tom said, "The first path that goes off this road between here an' the mission leads to Miz Brown's place."

"I know—I've been to visit her. Father doesn't see how such an old woman manages all by herself way out here. He thinks having the mission nearby will be a real blessing to her."

Tom looked at Amy in amazement. "Didn't you see her garden an' all them chickens? That ol' woman manages just fine." When Amy looked at him doubtfully, he added,

"She puts food by for winter an' trades eggs an' vegetables to Ol' Man Barnes for 'most anything else she needs. An' she's a granny woman, too."

"A granny woman?"

Tom nodded. "Ain't hardly a soul 'round here she didn't bring into the world."

"Oh, you mean she's a midwife," Amy said.

Tom seethed inwardly, wondering why she thought her word was better than the one everybody else used. They walked in silence for a few minutes, with Agamemnon plodding along behind them, before Amy said, "I don't see why you're taking Mrs. Brown buttermilk when she has her own cow. When I was there, I saw cow pies all around her fence."

"Cow pies?" Could she mean what he thought she did? Amy looked embarrassed. "You know. You see them all over the ground where cattle have been."

That *was* what she meant. Tom practically doubled over with laughter.

By now Amy's face was scarlet. "You still haven't answered my question," she said, glaring at Tom. "I want to know how come you're taking buttermilk to Mrs. Brown."

Thinking fast, Tom said, "Her cow's gone dry, that's how come."

Then he hollered, "Hoo-hoo!" He paused for a moment and repeated, "Hoo-hoo!"

Amy stared at him. "What was that all about?"

"You're supposed to holler before you git to somebody's place."

"You are? Why?"

"It's just the decent thing to do. It keeps you from surprisin' 'em."

The old woman met them at the gate, a smile lighting up her wizened face. "Pa sent you some buttermilk, since your cow's dry," Tom said, confidently lifting the jar from the sack. He knew she wouldn't give him away.

"You two can put it in the springhouse while I tie 'Memnon to the fence," Mrs. Brown said as she took the reins from Amy.

Inside the springhouse, Tom placed the jar in the icy water that flowed through a trough in the middle of the small, cool building. Amy looked at the basket of eggs on the shelf and then began lifting the lids and peering into the crocks cooling in the trough. Tom watched disapprovingly, surprised at how nosy she was.

Then they walked to the cabin, scattering the hens that were scratching in the yard. Inside, Mrs. Brown motioned them to the table, saying, "I never yet saw young'ns that couldn't eat a extry ham biscuit or two. These were left over from my boarder's breakfast."

"You have a boarder?" Amy asked, her eyes traveling around the tidy one-room cabin. "Where does he sleep?"

"Up in the loft where I dry my herbs. But he don't complain. Says he likes the smell of sage an' mint, an' that the board more 'n makes up for the room."

Tom finished his ham biscuit and thought enviously of Andy enjoying food like that two or three times a day.

As if reading his mind, the Widow Brown began bustling around. "I'll make up a packet of biscuits an' butter an' some fried chicken for you an' your pa. An' I'll put in a jar of them cucumber pickles you like so well, too."

"I have to go now," Amy said suddenly. "Thank you very much for the biscuit, Mrs. Brown." And without a word to Tom, she left.

From the cabin door, the Widow Brown watched Amy

untie Agamemnon, mount, and ride off. The old woman turned and looked thoughtfully at Tom, and then she came over to the table. Cupping his chin in her gnarled hand, she tipped his head so that she could look into his eyes.

"You listen to me, Tom," she said earnestly. "I know you're too young to be thinkin' about things like this just yet, but I might not be 'round to tell you, when the time comes. Don't you lose your heart to that li'l gal. Or to any flatlander, for that matter. Mark my words, nothin' but heartache would come of it. You hear me, boy?"

The Widow Brown released his chin, but she still held him with her eyes. "I hear you, Miz Brown," he whispered.

"There's a good lad," the old woman said, giving his shoulder a squeeze. "Now help yourself to another biscuit while I git them vittles from the springhouse."

Obediently, Tom took a biscuit, but he slipped it into his overalls pocket for later. Why had Mrs. Brown looked so serious when she warned him not to fall for Amy? (As if he would.) And what could he have done to make Amy go off without saying good-bye? And why did Mrs. Brown have to spoil his day by talking about when she might not be around?

After supper Tom cranked the sausage mill, grinding the sprouted corn kernels he'd spread on the shed roof that morning to dry in the sun. Already his arm was beginning to tire, but he kept on working. Pa needed the sprouted corn—he called it *malt* when it was ground—to start the mixture of cornmeal and water in the mash barrels fermenting.

Tom knew it would save a lot of time and trouble if Pa used yeast instead of malt and added sugar to his mash barrels, the way Eddie Jarvis and Hube Baker and all the other men did. It would take less cornmeal, too. But Pa prided himself on making pure corn whiskey the old-fashioned way—only he called it *traditional* instead of *old-fashioned*—and Tom was glad of it. Anybody could make sugar liquor, but making pure corn whiskey was a craft a person could be proud of.

Tom had just finished grinding the last of the malt and was closing the shed door behind him when he heard the sound of hooves on the rocky path. He was almost to the cabin when the preacher stormed through the gate and up to the porch to confront Pa.

"You lied. Yesterday you told my daughter that sack of corn would be used for cornmeal, but you made it into liquor and today you had this boy passing it off as buttermilk! How can you involve a child in this nefarious business?"

"Who do you think you're callin' a liar?"

Pa had risen to his feet and stood towering over Preacher Taylor, but the preacher held his ground. The air almost crackled with the men's anger. Tom feared for the preacher—nobody called June Higgins a liar and got away with it—until he had a flash of inspiration. He gave an ugly laugh and said, "You sure don't know much, Preacher Taylor."

Both men looked at him in surprise. "Two things everybody 'round here knows," Tom went on. "One is, my pa's no liar. The other is, you don't go from corn to whiskey in just a day or two. You've got to set your mash, an' then it takes a while to sprout some of the kernels an' grind 'em for malt, an' then you've gotta let the mash ferment for at least—"

"Enough!" Preacher Taylor said, holding up his hand. "I have no desire to learn how you manufacture your evil brew." Then he faced Pa again. "But I owe you an apology, Higgins. I was wrong to call you a liar."

Tom held his breath while Pa looked at the preacher for a long time, as if he were measuring the man's worth and weighing what his response should be. "See that you don't never do it again," Pa said at last. "Now set down in that rockin' chair and cool yourself off."

The preacher shook his head and declared, "It's my duty to destroy any liquor you have here so I can save the members of this community from the evils of drink."

"You won't find no likker here," Pa said. He winked at Tom and added, "Only drink I've got is a couple gallon of buttermilk."

Preacher Taylor's eyes lit up. "Where's your spring-house?" he demanded.

"Ain't got one. But there's a spring box out back. Tom, show him where it's at."

Pa was playing cat and mouse with the preacher, Tom realized as he led the way around the cabin. He wondered what they would find in the spring box.

"Aha!" the preacher said when he saw the five fruit jars immersed in the water alongside the crock that held the rest of Mrs. Brown's fried chicken and the butter.

As the man bent forward, Tom said, "Likker ain't white, Preacher Taylor."

"The boy's right, Preacher," Pa said. "Some folks call it white lightnin' 'cause it hits you like a bolt out of the blue, but it ain't really white at all."

"I know that. But I also know this can't be buttermilk, because you don't have a cow." Reaching for a jar, he said, "I'll bet you painted the inside of the glass."

"Wait," Pa commanded. "Tom, pick up the one closest to you an' unscrew the lid for the preacher."

Tom did as he was told and hid a grin when he saw that the jar was filled with a milky white liquid. "Want a taste?" he asked, looking up innocently.

The preacher made a face just like Amy had that morning, and then he turned to Pa. "I hope you don't really think you can fool me into believing the rest of these jars are full of buttermilk, too," he said scornfully. One by one, he lifted them from the spring box and opened them. Then, obviously disappointed to find that they all held the same white liquid, he stood up and said, "You've won this time, Higgins. But don't laugh too hard, because before I'm through here, these hills and hollows are going to be decent, law-abiding places for people to live."

"I don't laugh at folks who act accordin' to their convictions," Pa said, "but I don't much cotton to them that try an' make *me* act accordin' to their convictions."

The preacher pulled a handkerchief from his pocket and dried his hands. "Well, then," he said, "I guess we both know where we stand." And stuffing the handkerchief back in his pocket, he walked quickly around the cabin.

Tom looked up at Pa and asked, "How'd you know he was comin'? An' what did you put in them jars?"

"Use your head, boy. You told me yourself how nosy that li'l gal was down at Miz Brown's springhouse. What do you think she saw in them crocks?"

Closing his eyes, Tom tried to picture the contents of the crocks—fried chicken, milk, butter, maybe some clab-

ber cheese. His eyes popped open. So that was why Amy
had ignored him when she left. She knew he'd lied about
the Widow Brown's cow being dry.

"Bet it didn't take the preacher's gal that long to figure out what was goin' on," Pa said. "Anyhow," he
went on, self-satisfaction evident in his voice now, "I
mixed me some lime an' water till it looked enough like
buttermilk I wanted to drink it, poured it into them jars,
an' set back to wait for Preacher Taylor to come ridin' up
here."

"What's he gonna do next, Pa?"

"I don't know, boy, but whatever it is, you can bet I'm
gonna be ready for him."

Tom didn't doubt that for a minute. The preacher didn't
stand a chance against his pa.

7

"That's him—he said he'd holler." Tom tried to keep the
excitement out of his voice. He ran to the gate to meet
Andy, but Pa kept his place on the bench.

Tom greeted their guest and escorted him to the porch.
"This here's my pa," he said proudly as Andy stooped to
keep from bumping his head on the low porch roof.

"So you've come to hear a story," Pa said, standing up.

"That's right," Andy said as they shook hands.

"Wal, have a seat in that there rocker, an' we'll discuss
it," Pa said, lowering himself onto the bench again.

Tom frowned. What was there to discuss?

Pa gave Andy an appraising look and said, "I hope you don't expect me to give my tales away without gittin' nothin' in return."

Andy looked surprised. "What did you have in mind?"

"A swap. For every tale I tell, you tell one. An' you can start, since you're a guest."

Good for Pa, Tom thought, reaching into his pocket for his whittling knife. "Do you know the one about the kings, Andy?" he asked hopefully.

"Which kings do you mean?"

"Agamemnon and Odysseus," Tom said, wondering how many kings there were.

"The Iliad!" Andy exclaimed. "Sure, I know that one. It's the story of how the Greek kings and their men fought a war with the Trojans over Helen, the beautiful queen who had been stolen away from her husband by a prince from Troy."

Tom shaved a curl of wood from the ear of the fox he was carving. At least his ma hadn't been stolen away by another man, he thought. Pa wouldn't have stood for that any more than those kings did. But it would have been easier for *him* to understand than her leaving of her own free will. And leaving him behind. Suddenly catching the name Agamemnon, Tom turned his attention to Andy.

The sun was low by the time Andy leaned back and said, "This is a good stopping place—it's much too long a story for one night." He reached into his hip pocket and drew out a flask. After he drank, he passed the flask to Pa and said, "Try this. You won't find any better."

Pa reached for it and took a swallow. "You're right," he agreed. "You won't find no better. Where'd you git this here whiskey?"

"Whiskey? That's buttermilk. I found it in Mrs. Brown's springhouse."

Tom grinned as he shaved away a bit of wood from his fox's tail. Andy sure was different from Preacher Taylor.

Pa wiped his mouth with his sleeve and handed back the flask. "Wal," he said, "my story happened a long time ago, too—back in my grandpap's day. But it happened right here in this holler. An' my story has a king, not a king with a army, but a man the neighbors all looked to as a leader. Sometimes folks called him King Britten, but even when they was callin' him Josiah, they knew better 'n to cross him."

"Folks sometimes call Pa King Higgins," Tom said. "Did you know that, Andy?"

"You know better 'n to interrupt my story, boy," Pa growled.

Tom bent over his carving and muttered "Sorry," but he knew Pa hadn't really minded the interruption.

The next evening Andy came to the cabin again, and this time he had a notebook with him. "Later I'm going to write down your story in this," he explained when he saw Tom and Pa looking at it. He rocked quietly for a moment and then picked up the story of the Greek kings where he'd left off the night before. Tom listened, entranced, as Andy's voice rose and fell, sometimes tense with excitement, sometimes almost a whisper.

Finally, Andy stopped and reached for the jar of moonshine Pa passed him. After he drank, he handed the jar back to Pa and said, "I'll be writing down your story, June, but don't worry about whether I'm keeping up. I won't have any trouble at all."

Pa took a swallow from the jar and screwed the lid back on, and Tom couldn't tell whether he was pleased or nervous about all this.

"Actually, what I'm gonna tell you tonight ain't really a tale," Pa said. "It's somethin' that happened to me a couple years back. It was a night in late October, with a big ol' moon a-hangin' in the sky all round an' yaller, an' I thought to myself, Now this is a night for a coon hunt if I ever saw one. So I got my gun an' called my dog Blue, an' off I went."

A little shiver of anticipation ran down Tom's spine. Pa's coon hunt stories were among his best. The Jack tales and the King Britten stories Pa had learned years ago from his uncle, but the coon hunt stories were his very own.

"Wal, directly I met Cat Johnson on the path an' I say, 'Hey Cat! Git your ol' hound dog an' your gun.' Pretty soon we had us a group of five or six men, each of us with one of the finest dogs that ever walked these woods, an' . . ."

Tom was putting the finishing touches on his fox carving when Pa came to the end of the story. "Then, just as the moon went behind a cloud, we heard somethin' comin' up Jenkins Branch. We knew it was fearful big, from the splashin' it was makin'. An' as it came closer, the trees whipped to and fro like in a great wind, but there wasn't even a breeze stirrin', an' the dogs tucked their tails between their legs an' whimpered. Other 'n that, the only sound was that terrible splashin', gittin' closer and closer to us. By now, of course, we was all behind that big boulder beside the branch, peerin' over the top.

"Then all of a sudden the moon came out from behind that cloud an' it seemed 'most light as day, an' we could see the water splashin' an' churnin' in the branch—but there was nothin' there! An' then the splashin' an' churnin' stopped right opposite the boulder we was behind. The trees stopped their wavin', too. Wal, by then we'd all ducked down behind the boulder, but I peered 'round the side of it, an' what do you think I seen?"

"What?" breathed Tom. He hadn't heard this tale before.

"I seen wet footprints appear on the steppin' stones. *Huge* wet footprints, an' there was nary a creature making 'em!"

Tom frowned. He knew the boulder Pa was talking about, but there weren't any stepping stones. Just the footlog.

"An' while I watched, one by one, them steppin' stones just sank right down into the water. Whatever made them footprints was so heavy it pushed 'em clean down in the mud so's they disappeared. We never did know what it was we didn't see, but nobody doubted we didn't see it, 'cause them steppin' stones was gone. An' they still are. Ain't that right, Tom?"

Tom nodded, wondering if Andy would think about Pa's story when he crossed there on his way back to the Widow Brown's cabin. Would he shine that fancy flashlight of his all up and down the branch before he stepped onto the footlog?

Tom watched the man close his notebook and clip his pencil into his shirt pocket, and suddenly he wished he could write. He wondered why somebody didn't tell Preacher Taylor that if he really wanted to help the people in these hills, he'd hurry up and build that school.

8

Tom couldn't remember when the trip to the settlement had seemed to take so long. For the hundredth time, he glanced back to make sure the two sacks Pa had knotted together for him to drape across Ol' Sal's back were still safely in place.

He wished he hadn't volunteered to take Pa's whiskey to the store. He should have just walked down and told Ol' Man Barnes that Pa wouldn't be able to make his delivery tonight because he'd twisted his ankle. But instead he'd offered to take the whiskey two miles down the mountain, pretending the painted jars were filled with buttermilk.

The clank of the jars made Tom nervous, and he tried to reassure himself that no one would suspect they weren't really full of buttermilk. After all, delivering a batch of moonshine wasn't a boy's job, and it wasn't something you did in broad daylight, either.

It seemed like a long time before Tom passed the cabins scattered along the trail near the mouth of the hollow. He drew a deep breath, relieved that his trip would soon be over. When he came into the settlement, he saw a magnificent black horse tied in front of the store. Several men were admiring it, and without thinking, Tom hurried to join them.

As he approached, the men turned toward him. One look at their faces when they heard the clanking of jars in the sacks slung across Ol' Sal's back told Tom that the powerful horse belonged to a revenuer. And as if to confirm this, he heard two shots from the direction of the Rigsbys' house. Lonny must have been at the store with his pa and slipped home to fire the signal when the revenuer arrived.

Tom's mouth went dry. What should he do now? As he hesitated, a portly stranger with steel-gray hair came out of the store and glanced around. When the man's eyes fell on Tom, he knew he had no choice, so he took a deep breath and started forward again. With trembling fingers, he tied Ol' Sal to the porch rail, and then he joined the group around the sleek black horse. He could feel the stranger's eyes on him as he greeted the men and ran his hand along the animal's neck.

Then, trying to look like a boy who was bringing buttermilk to trade at the store, Tom untied the sacks, left one on the ground, and picked up the other. The jars inside clanked together as he hung the sack over his shoulder, and the stranger came down the steps of the store and said, "I'll give you a hand with that." But instead of picking up the second sack, he began to open it.

His heart pounding, Tom started up the steps to the store. "It's easier to carry them jars if you leave 'em in the sack," he said over his shoulder. The men standing around the horse stared at him, and when the stranger followed him inside, Ol' Man Barnes stared, too. Beads of sweat gathered on the storekeeper's forehead.

"I've brought some buttermilk for you to sell in town tomorrow, Mr. Barnes," Tom said, hoisting his sack onto the counter. He thought his voice sounded unnaturally loud in the suddenly quiet store. "There's five jars in each sack," he went on, rolling down the top to show the two-quart jars.

Ol' Man Barnes drew a deep breath and reached for his ledger. "That's twice two-and-a-half gallon, five altogether," he said, his voice quavering. "Put it in the springhouse while I record it."

"Thanks for carryin' that in for me, mister," Tom said to the stranger. As Tom headed toward the back door with his load, he glanced behind him and saw with relief that the man had lost interest in his jars.

Outside, his knees almost buckling under him, Tom managed to stumble to the springhouse and open the door. The rush of cool air made him shiver as he ducked inside. He put the jars in the trough of cold water, just as if they really were full of buttermilk, and then, suddenly aware of how dry his mouth was, he reached for the dipper and drank. Unsteadily, he got to his feet and headed back to the store for the second sack.

An hour later, as he approached the cabin, Tom saw that Pa hadn't moved from the rocking chair on the porch, where he sat with his foot propped up on a wooden box. All the way home, Tom had rehearsed how he'd tell Pa about his narrow escape at the store. But now, seeing the stony expression on Pa's face, he wished he didn't have to say anything about what had happened. He knew, though, that the story was bound to be the talk of the hollow for days, and that Pa had better hear it from him first.

Tom slid off Ol' Sal's back, and after he turned her into the pasture and hung the bridle on its peg in the shed, he squared his shoulders and walked to the porch.

"What took you so long?" Pa asked irritably.

"I had a little trouble," Tom admitted. And then he described his encounter with the revenuer.

"That was a chance we hadn't ought to of took," Pa said. "From now on, if I can't make the delivery, it just don't git made. You understand?"

Tom nodded. "I understand," he said. He wasn't about to argue—he'd been half scared to death down at the store, and he had no desire to go through anything like that again. But he was disappointed that Pa hadn't said a word about how well he'd handled the situation.

"Dadburn preacher," Pa muttered. "Never had all this trouble before he came here. Him an' that li'l gal of his. Now c'mon, boy," he said, bracing himself with his stick as he struggled to his feet. "We got work to do."

"What kind of work, Pa?" Tom asked, puzzled. Pa leaned on his stick and asked, "Just how long d'you think it'll be before that revenuer finds his way up here? Wal, when he does, we're gonna look so innocent he decides he's wastin' his time. Now git a shovel."

While Pa watched, Tom buried the last two jars of moonshine in the potato patch. Then he listened intently to Pa's plan and set off for the Widow Brown's cabin.

To his relief, he didn't meet Amy on the way. This was one time he definitely didn't want her walking with him. He was dismayed when he came in sight of the cabin and saw Agamemnon tied to the fence. Everything was going wrong today! Well, he'd just have to wait till Amy left before he got what Pa had sent him for, Tom thought as he gave a holler.

Both Mrs. Brown and Amy seemed pleased to see him, but when he joined them on the porch Amy frowned and asked, "What are those sacks for?"

"Why, they're for carryin' jars of buttermilk," Tom said, giving the Widow Brown an exaggerated wink.

Amy's face flushed, and she got to her feet. Ignoring Tom, she turned to Mrs. Brown and said, "I'll come visit you again sometime when you don't have other company."

As Amy rode off, Mrs. Brown gave Tom a mischievous look and said, "She sure didn't much appreciate you bringin' up the subject of buttermilk." Chuckling, she added, "Wish I could of seen her pa openin' all them jars in June's spring box. Still, I don't rightly know why you wanted to rile her like that."

"I didn't want to rile her—I just didn't want her 'round while I was gittin' what I came for," Tom said uncomfortably.

"I was hopin' you came for to bring me some whiskey. Why *did* you come? Not that I ain't pleased to see you anytime at all, you understand."

"Can you let me have a jar of buttermilk? Real buttermilk?"

The Widow Brown stood up and said, "Sure can—an' some butter an' fresh-baked bread, too. Anything else you'd like to have? I see you brought two sacks."

Tom followed her out the gate. "While you're gittin' the buttermilk an' all, I'll just fill the other sack with cow pies, long as that's all right with you," he said, putting a serious look on his face.

"Cow pies?" The old woman peered at him, her wrinkled forehead furrowed into a frown. "I don't think I got no cow pies, Tom."

Struggling to keep a straight face, Tom gestured to the flat, round splats of dried cow manure on the ground outside the fence. "Sure you do, Miz Brown—an' they're just what Pa and I need."

She stared at him for a moment before she started toward the springhouse. "Help yourself, boy," she said over her shoulder. "You just help yourself."

Grinning now, Tom began filling the sack with the dried manure. When Mrs. Brown came back, he'd tell her what he was going to do with it, and they'd have a good laugh.

9

Tom and Pa were just finishing their fried potatoes and salt pork that evening when they heard the gate creak. Tom started to get up, but Pa growled, "Set down, boy." Soon a man's shape was silhouetted in the doorway.

"Who's there?" Pa challenged.

"P. D. Hudson, federal agent."

"What is it you want, Petey?" Pa asked, standing up.

Without answering, the revenuer came inside, and a stolid young man he didn't bother to introduce took his place in the doorway. Hudson looked around, blinking to accustom his eyes to the dimness of the small cabin. A glimmer of recognition crossed his face when he saw Tom.

The revenuer's eyes lingered on the rifle hanging over the huge fireplace, moved first to Tom's carved chipmunk and the dust-covered Bible on the mantel, then to the iron skillet resting on the hearth. He showed no interest in the two sturdy stools, but he seemed to be memorizing every detail of the rocking chair Pa had made of maple and hickory wood. Finally turning away, he glanced at Pa's bed and the blanket chest and looked with interest at the homemade ladder nailed to the back wall below a square hole in the ceiling. At last, his gaze came to rest on the remains of the evening meal.

Tom wished they had a tablecloth like Mrs. Brown's. And that Pa had straightened and smoothed his quilt like she did, instead of leaving it in a rumpled heap.

"I asked you what it is you want, Petey," Pa said, leaning on his stick and moving closer to the revenuer. Tom saw the man in the doorway watching tensely.

"I've been told you have a still around here, and—"

"Of course I'm still around here," Pa said impatiently. "I've lived in this here cabin since I was born, an' there's been no reason to leave."

But the revenuer was not one to be toyed with. "Mr. Higgins," he said, "I've had a report that you're making whiskey back in these hills, and I've come to investigate. I have a warrant to search these premises for evidence."

Pa let his mouth drop open. "Makin' whiskey! How could anybody say such a thing? You go right ahead an' investigate, Petey, an' I'll help you all I can. I want my named cleared."

The revenuer looked surprised—and a little suspicious. "Then I'll start by looking around in here."

"Look all you want, inside an' out," Pa said. "I can guarantee you won't find a drop of whiskey on this place."

If Tom hadn't been so nervous, he would have laughed at Pa's clever choice of words. But seeing the revenuer again brought back some of the fear he'd felt at the store that morning.

After the man had looked under the bed and in the blanket chest, Pa said, "Tom, take Petey on up to the loft."

Nimbly, Tom climbed the ladder and scrambled through the hole into the low-ceilinged loft where he slept. Hudson turned to his companion and said, "Cory, climb up there and have a look."

Moments later, Cory was beside Tom. He looked around the loft, kicked once or twice at the straw-tick mattress, and squatted down to peer inside the box where Tom kept his treasures—his slingshot, a bag of marbles, the birds and animals he'd carved, and the rattles from the snake Agamemnon had trampled. Picking up one of the bird carvings, Cory studied it a moment before he dropped it back into the box. Then he lowered himself through the hole in the loft floor, feeling for the ladder with his foot.

Tom dropped to the cabin floor in time to see Cory glance in Hudson's direction and shake his head as he crossed the room to take his place at the door.

"Show me around outside now," Hudson ordered Tom. Silently, Cory stepped aside to let the others pass, and then he fell into step behind Pa, who was stumping along with his stick. From the corner of his eye, Tom saw a movement in the orchard and caught his breath. How many revenuers were there?

At the spring box, Hudson unscrewed the lid from the jar of buttermilk Tom had gotten from the Widow Brown that afternoon and sniffed suspiciously. Pouring a few drops onto his finger, he tasted it. Then, rising to his feet, he headed for the woodpile. "Check this, Cory," he said to his partner. He watched impassively while the man tossed the logs aside. Then he pointed at the shed that served as Ol' Sal's stable and asked, "What's that building?"

"The boy will show you soon as you stack that there wood back up," Pa said.

The revenuer pointed first to his silent helper and then to the scattered logs, and without changing his expression, the other man set to work.

After Hudson had satisfied himself that there was no moonshine in the shed, Tom pointed at the corncrib and asked, "Ain't you gonna look in there?"

"Bring me a hoe," the revenuer said.

Tom brought one from the toolshed and watched, disappointed, while Cory poked the handle into the stored corn over and over again. He'd hoped the man would toss out the ears and then have to gather them all up.

Hudson headed toward the toolshed, motioning for Cory to follow him. Inside, he glanced first at the tools and Pa's traps hanging on the walls and then at the cider press in one corner and the hog-scalding barrel with the sausage mill and butchering equipment inside it in another corner. He pointed to the barrel, and Cory started lifting things out, one by one.

Tom's heart began to pound. He hadn't cleaned the sausage mill after he'd ground the malt in it! Would his carelessness provide the revenuers with proof that Pa was making whiskey? Nobody but a moonshiner would grind sprouted grain.

Cory had the sausage mill in his hands when Tom heard Andy's holler. The revenuers exchanged glances, and Hudson said, "Sounds like some kind of signal."

"That's our friend Andy, comin' up to swap tales," Tom said.

Ignoring him, Hudson said, "There's nothing here. Come on, let's go see who that is." Tom and Pa followed the revenuers out of the shed and around the cabin in time to see Andy come into the yard.

Hudson went to meet him. "I'm P. D. Hudson, federal agent."

Andy shook hands with him. "Paul Anderson. I'm a folklorist."

"A folklorist?" Hudson repeated suspiciously.

Nodding, Andy showed him his notebook. "I make notes about mountain customs and record traditional tales and ballads. June Higgins is the finest storyteller I know of." Andy turned to Pa and said, "By the way, June, I met Preacher Taylor on my way up here and he sent you his regards."

"Ah, yes, the preacher who's going to rid these hills of the evils of drink," Hudson said bitterly. "It'll be a long time before he gets me back to this God-forsaken mountain again with his wild imaginings." Nodding to Pa and Andy, he stalked out the gate, with Cory right behind him.

The others watched them go. "It must have been their footprints I saw going into the woods where that little creek crosses the path," Andy mused.

"Must of been," Pa said noncommittally.

That was why Pa had insisted that they remove every trace of evidence that a still had been set up at the old site, Tom realized. If those revenuers had found so much as a piece of charred wood, they wouldn't have thought the preacher imagined Pa was a moonshiner. Tom vowed that when he was a man, he'd make sure his son always knew the reason for what he did, so the boy would understand why it was important.

As they started toward the porch, Andy said, "Now I see why Mrs. Brown's cow looked so tired at milking time this evening."

"Why's that?" asked Tom.

"Well, it's obvious she'd wandered all the way up here." Andy gestured to the dried manure Tom had scattered outside the fence and along the edge of the rocky pasture where Ol' Sal was grazing.

Scornfully, Pa said, "I knowed once them city fellers saw that, they'd never notice there weren't no barn or cow shed—an' nary a churn on the place."

Tom remembered how confident he'd felt once he had made sure the revenuer would see signs of the cows that produced the "buttermilk" he'd taken to the store. He'd never thought about a churn, either. Quickly changing the subject, Tom turned to Andy and asked, "Are you gonna tell us some more about them Greek kings tonight?"

When Andy nodded and reached for his pipe, Tom pulled out his whittling knife and the bird he was carving. Someday, he thought, he'd make a tale out of how he'd tricked that revenuer down at the store this morning and helped Pa trick him again tonight.

10

Tom was about to go into the store for the twists of chewing tobacco Pa had sent him for when Cat Johnson called, "Hey, Tom! Look what I got here."

Curious, Tom waited while Cat came up onto the store porch. Reaching into his sack, Cat lifted out a tan and white puppy. The minute he set her down, she scampered toward Tom and began to sniff his feet. Tom wiggled his toes and the little dog backed up so fast she almost fell over. Grinning, Tom sat down on the step, and the puppy clambered into his lap. Resting her paws on Tom's chest, she tried to lick his face. Tom scooped the puppy up and held her close, feeling the rapid beat of her heart.

While Cat Johnson chatted with the other men on the store porch, Tom played with the puppy. He put her down when Cat was ready to leave, but she just climbed back into his lap and began to nibble on his fingers.

Cat bent over to pick her up, and as he put her into his sack he shook his head and said, "Seems a shame to have to drown such a fine animal, don't it?" He slung the sack over his shoulder and started toward the mill pond.

"Wait!" Tom cried, hurrying after him. "How come you're gonna drown her?"

"She's the runt of the litter an' don't nobody want her," Cat said over his shoulder.

Catching up to him, Tom asked, "What about Miz Brown?"

"She said she don't need no puppy chasin' after them hens of hers," Cat said. "An', Tom, I'd be much obliged if you didn't let on to my boys that I had to kill this pup. I'd rather let 'em think somebody from over in Ox Gore Holler took her."

Even though Tom knew that people drowned unwanted kittens and puppies, he'd never thought much about it. But how could anyone drown *this* puppy?

"Here," Cat said, thrusting the sack at Tom, "hold it open while I put that big ol' rock in with her so she'll sink right away an' won't struggle as long." He bent to pick up the rock.

"No!" Tom cried, clutching the sack to his chest. "I'll take her, Mr. Johnson."

"What you gonna name your new dog?" an old man called from the store porch.

"Princess," Tom called back as the puppy clawed her way out of the mouth of the sack and pressed her cold nose against his neck. He cradled her against him and whispered, "You're beautiful, you know that?" To his delight, Princess snuggled into the crook of his arm, gave a squeaky yawn, and closed her eyes. A warm feeling stole over Tom, and his heart swelled as he looked down at her. Already, Princess trusted him.

He started up the trail, feeling the puppy's warm breath on his skin. He didn't care that his arm was already beginning to tire from her weight. It wasn't until he was halfway home that Princess stirred and woke. Tom shifted her to his other arm and said, "One day soon, you'll be big enough to walk along with me. An' then you'll foller me everywhere I go, won't you?" He held her against his cheek and she wiggled ecstatically.

Finally, back at the cabin, Tom put Princess on the ground, and she followed him to the spring, where they both drank. Then she sat back on her haunches, looked up at Tom expectantly, and gave one yap.

"You're hungry, ain't you?" he said. In the cabin, he scraped some burnt corn bread from the skillet, but the little dog just sniffed it and looked up at him again. Not knowing what else to do, he went to the spring box and opened the crock where the last of Mrs. Brown's fried chicken was stored. Princess began to wag her tail and dance about, but when Tom set the meat in front of her, she just licked it and then looked up at him.

He was intent on cutting off bits of chicken and hand feeding them to the puppy when Pa's voice startled him. "Whose mutt is that? An' where's them tobacco twists you was supposed to git me?"

Tom grabbed the puppy and scrambled to his feet. "She's mine," he said, his stomach lurching as he realized he'd forgotten the tobacco. "Cat Johnson gave her to me."

Pa looked from Tom to the dog to the scraps of meat. "Wal, you can just give her right back to him. I don't need no extra mouth to feed."

"But, Pa! I can't take her back—Cat was gonna drown her!"

Pa scowled at Tom and said, "I suppose he told you she's the runt of the litter an' asked you to hold the sack while he found him a big rock to weigh it down with, didn't he? An' you fell for that ol' trick of his."

Tom felt his face growing hot. "Can't I keep her anyway? Please?" he asked, swallowing his pride. "I—I *need* her."

"Need her! What for, to give you another excuse to forgit to do what you're told?" Pa glowered at Tom. "Now go on back to the store for my tobacco, an' git rid of that mutt before you come home, you hear?"

His eyes downcast, Tom nodded. "I hear," he said tonelessly. Holding Princess close to him, he started toward the settlement. Pa could be downright mean. He didn't care about Princess, and he probably didn't really care about *him*—not enough to let him keep his puppy, anyway.

Hugging Princess closer to him, Tom decided he didn't really mind that Cat Johnson had tricked him. Maybe Cat could use the same trick to find someone else to take Princess, he thought. But probably he'd just drown her and not think twice about it.

Tom hesitated when he came to the path that led to the footlog. He hadn't seen Amy since the day he'd gone to Mrs. Brown's cabin for the "cow pies." He hoped she wasn't still angry with him. Looking down into the puppy's trusting eyes, Tom headed for the mission. Part of him was in a hurry to find out if Amy would take Princess, but part of him wanted to stretch out the little time he had left with her.

From the edge of the clearing around the mission house, Tom saw Amy sitting on the porch, reading. He called to her, and when she put down her book and ran to meet him, he set Princess on the ground. He watched miserably as the puppy gamboled toward Amy.

Amy gave a little cry and picked up Princess. "What a sweet puppy. Is she yours?"

Taking a deep breath, Tom said, "She was, but you can have her." At least Amy wasn't mad at him anymore.

"I couldn't possibly take your dog, Tom," she said, looking shocked.

"You gotta take her!" he cried. "Pa won't let me keep her, an' if I give her back to Cat Johnson, he's gonna drown her."

At that moment, Mrs. Taylor joined them. She greeted Tom warmly when Amy introduced them, and then she admired Princess.

"May I keep her, Mother?" Amy asked, hugging the little dog. "Please?"

Mrs. Taylor shook her head. "Absolutely not, Amy. You know how your father feels about pets," she said firmly.

"But, Mother! Tom's father won't let him have her, and if I can't keep her, she'll be drowned!"

Tom looked pleadingly at Mrs. Taylor. "Please, ma'am?" He'd never beg for himself, but this was different.

Mrs. Taylor looked from Tom to Princess and then turned to her daughter. "You know you can't have a dog, Amy," she said. "But I think we could arrange for Tom to keep Princess here if you're willing to take care of her."

Tom's knees went weak with relief and he drew a shaky breath. He couldn't trust himself to speak, so he just nodded when Mrs. Taylor said, "You'll come down to see your dog whenever you can, won't you, Tom?"

Taking Princess from Amy, he buried his face in her puppy-soft fur one last time. Then he handed her back and said, "You'd best hold her so she don't foller me."

Tom gave Mrs. Taylor a look of gratitude and set off along the old wagon road, headed for the settlement. Princess was safe, and he could see her whenever he wanted to. But he might have been able to keep her if he hadn't made Pa angry by forgetting the tobacco twists. And if he hadn't been caught feeding her the chicken. And if he'd asked if he could keep her instead of telling Pa she was his dog.

When Tom came to the Widow Brown's path, he barely

hesitated before turning toward her cabin. Pa would just have to wait a little longer for his tobacco. A few minutes later, Tom was drinking a glass of cold buttermilk and pouring out his story. When he finished, Mrs. Brown said, "I sure wish you could of kept that pretty li'l dog, Tom. But you didn't have her long enough to miss her all that much. An' you can walk down to see her as often as you want."

Tom stared glumly at the ground. He knew Mrs. Brown was right, but that wasn't what he'd wanted to hear.

"Now, you ain't gonna sit here feelin' sorry for yourself, are you, Tom?" she chided gently.

" 'Course not," he said, embarrassed to realize that was exactly what he was doing. "I'm gonna git on over to the store an' back up that mountain before Pa decides I forgot his tobacco again."

If Pa asked, he'd tell him he gave the puppy to Amy, Tom decided, because no matter what Mrs. Taylor said, and no matter what he wished, Princess wasn't his dog anymore. But he didn't mind pretending she was, if that was the way Mrs. Taylor wanted it.

11

Growing the corn was the worst part of making whiskey, Tom thought as he helped Pa hoe. It would be a lot less work if Pa bought his cornmeal from the miller, but he insisted that the white corn he grew made better whiskey than the yellow corn most people planted. Tom wiped the sweat off his forehead with the back of his hand and wondered how soon he dared make another trip to the spring. And how long he dared take for that trip.

Pa straightened up and said, "Somebody's comin'."

They waited expectantly, and when the preacher rode up, Tom followed Pa over to the fence. Pa's twisted ankle was completely healed now, Tom noticed.

"I need your help, Higgins," the preacher said, reining in Odysseus and pulling out a handkerchief to mop his sweaty face.

"Why would I want to help you?" Pa asked testily. "Ever since you came here you been causin' me trouble. Even sent the federal law up here after me last week."

The preacher's shoulders slumped. "Then I'll have failed," he said. "Failed to bring religion and education into these hills."

Education! Tom looked pleadingly at Pa, but his father seemed intent on avoiding his eyes. "K-e-r-o-s-e-n-e," Tom spelled under his breath. Preacher Taylor looked at him strangely, but Tom didn't care.

Pa shifted a wad of tobacco to his other cheek and demanded, "Just what makes you think I can help you?"

"The storekeeper told me you were a leader around here. He said some people even call you King Higgins. I want you to use your influence to get the men to help me build the mission's schoolhouse-chapel." The preacher mopped his face again. "I think that neighbor of yours, Hube Baker, has turned everyone against me."

Pa snorted. "He didn't have to turn nobody against you, 'cause they always *was* against you. Hube's right peeved with you, but he don't have no influence on folks."

"But why would Mr. Baker be peeved with me?"

When Pa didn't answer, Tom said, "He probably thinks you had somethin' to do with the sheriff an' his deputies catchin' him carryin' his jars of whiskey home from the still. Everybody knows the sheriff don't come back in here 'less he's had a complaint, an' Hube was caught right after you saw him loadin' that hundred-pound sack of sugar onto his ol' mule down at the store."

The preacher looked surprised. "You must be mistaken, Tom—Mr. Baker's not in jail. I saw him when I rode by his cabin on my way up here."

" 'Course he ain't in jail," Pa said impatiently. "Court day's not for nearly two weeks."

"But who put up his bond?"

Tom and Pa looked at the preacher blankly, and he tried again. "Who left money with the court to make sure he shows up for the trial?"

" 'Round here, it's a matter of honor," Pa said stiffly. "Honor, an' respect for the law."

Tom added, "A feller over in Ox Gore Holler killed his neighbor in a fight last year when they was both drunk, an' all the sheriff had to do was send word with Ol' Man Barnes. When that feller heard the sheriff had a warrant on him, he walked to town an' turned hisself in."

Preacher Taylor stared down at them. "That's hard to believe," he said slowly. "How can people have that kind of respect for the law and still flout Prohibition?"

"Easy," Pa said. "Murder an' stealin' have always been against the law. Makin' whiskey h'ain't. Writin' a law against somethin' don't make it wrong."

"But it's the law of the land," the preacher protested, "and—"

"It ain't the law of this here land of mine," Pa inter-

69

rupted, emphasizing his point by pounding his hoe on the ground. "Ain't nobody can tell me what to do with corn I grow on my own property. What difference does it make whether I turn it into corn bread or corn whiskey?"

"It makes a lot of difference," Preacher Taylor said, leaning forward in his saddle. "Corn bread doesn't make men kill each other in drunken brawls. Whiskey does. Corn bread doesn't make men beat their wives and children. Whiskey does. Buying corn bread feeds the hungry. Buying whiskey takes food out of their mouths. Corn bread—"

Tom caught his breath as Pa held up his hand and said wearily, "Save your sermon 'til you get that schoolhouse-chapel built, Preacher."

"Does this mean—?"

"I can't speak for the others, but you let me know when you're ready to start work, an' I'll be there."

It was all Tom could do not to cheer. If Pa worked on the schoolhouse-chapel, the other men would, too.

The preacher's face lit up with an almost boyish smile. "You mean that? How long do you think it will take to build it? I hate not being able to hold Sunday services."

Pa looked at him as if he were crazy. "You don't need no church for Sunday services," he said scornfully.

"But there isn't any building large enough to hold all the people," Preacher Taylor protested.

Pa spit a stream of tobacco juice past Odysseus's nose. "Ain't never had no buildin' before. Any time a preacher showed up an' wanted to hold services, we built a brush tabernacle for him."

Preacher Taylor frowned. "A brush tabernacle?"

This time Tom didn't wait to give Pa a chance to explain. "You put up a wood frame an' cover the top an' sides with branches an' vines to keep off the sun, an' you roll logs underneath it for folks to sit on," he said eagerly. "It don't take long to make one."

"Then why hasn't anybody built a brush tabernacle so *I* can hold services? What do you people think I came here for?" the preacher asked.

Pa gave him an appraising look. "Far as we could tell, you came here to rid these hills of the evils of moonshine likker."

"There's a lot more to my mission here than promoting abstinence from beverage alcohol," the preacher said. He looked a little embarrassed.

"That so?" Pa asked, leaning on his hoe and grinning. "Couldn't prove it by me."

The preacher's face reddened, and he quoted, " 'How then shall they call on Him in whom they have not believed? And how shall they believe in Him of whom they have not heard? And how shall they hear without a preacher?' " Then he looked down at Tom. "Today's Thursday. Think you can spread the word so that brush tabernacle's ready by Sunday morning?"

"Sure can!" Tom said enthusiastically. Folks liked any kind of community gathering.

"Good," the preacher said. "Then we don't have to be in such a hurry to start on the schoolhouse-chapel. The end of September's still a long way off."

"What's September got to do with it?"

Preacher Taylor looked surprised that Pa had asked. "That's when school starts."

"When I was a boy, we had a summer term a couple

of times in a ol' cabin nobody used," Pa said. "It don't make no sense to have these young'ns wait till September to start school. Besides, you'll have a easier time findin' a teacher now."

"My wife will be the teacher," the preacher said, "but I think you're right about not waiting till fall. When can you get started on the building? I don't want to order more lumber till the last minute." As if to himself, he added, "Replacing those boards that burned is such a needless expense."

The preacher's wife would be his teacher! Tom was thinking about how hard he'd work for her when Pa's words shook him out of his daydream.

"I think I know somebody who'd make a contribution of cash money to pay for that lumber," Pa said.

Preacher Taylor's eyes widened. "You do?"

" 'Deed I do," Pa said, "an' it's Eddie Jarvis."

Tom brushed a fly off Odysseus's nose, glad Pa had finally decided how to deal with Eddie. A man couldn't be allowed to get away with burning somebody out.

"You really think Mr. Jarvis will do that?" the preacher asked eagerly.

"He will if he knows King Higgins said he would. Stop in at the store an' leave a message for Eddie. Have Ol' Man Barnes tell him King Higgins said he knew Eddie'd be happy to pay the cost of replacin' the preacher's lumber that was burned."

"That seems like an awfully roundabout way to do things," the preacher said. "I'll just ride up to Mr. Jarvis's cabin and—"

"You can't do that!" Tom interrupted, alarmed. "Ain't nobody goes up there."

"Eddie Jarvis likes his privacy," Pa said. " 'Round here, we respect that."

Preacher Taylor frowned and said, "Maybe your way's best at that, Higgins. I've never been able to get past that dog he keeps tied in his yard."

Tom was still reeling with surprise that the preacher had actually gone up to Eddie's place and lived to tell about it when he realized Pa was speaking.

"A man over in Ox Gore Holler has a sawmill," Pa said, "an' I think you'd do better dealin' with him instead of the lumberyard in town."

"I'll show you the sketch of what I want and let you take care of ordering whatever you'll need, Higgins," the preacher said. "You know a lot more about this sort of thing than I do." He gave a flick of the reins, and Odysseus tossed his head and started back down the trail.

As Tom and Pa began to hoe the corn again, Tom said, "You know what Preacher Taylor said about the whiskey? I think he's right. Whenever somethin' bad happens 'round here, you can bet somebody was drunk."

"You think that means we should be selling corn *bread* instead of corn *whiskey?*" Pa asked.

Tom heard the challenge in Pa's voice. " 'Course not," he said quickly. "Moonshiners don't make corn bread." But that don't change the truth of what the preacher said, he added silently.

12

It was more than a week later when Tom set off to pick blackberries to trade at the store. Half a mile down the trail he passed the Bakers' cabin and saw Hube Baker leaning back in his chair with his feet on the porch railing while his wife, Emma, hoed the garden patch.

"Heard about how you fooled the federal law down at the store the other day," Hube called. "You done good, Tom."

"Thanks, Mr. Baker," Tom called back. He *had* done good, he thought, and it should have been Pa, not Hube, who told him so. Why was Pa so hard to please? "I guess there ain't no answer to that one," Tom muttered as he continued down the trail.

Halfway to the settlement he stopped at the best bramble patch he knew of and began to pick, swearing when a briar caught him on the hand and tiny drops of blood beaded up along the scratch. Tom worked quickly, and by the time he'd reached the end of the berry patch, his basket was full. That should be enough to trade for some more marbles, Tom decided as he started downhill again.

A short time later, he was watching the storekeeper carefully pour the berries into small square boxes to sell in Buckton the next day. They both looked up as a woman came into the store carrying a small child on her hip.

"I heard there was some excitement here the other day when you brought your pa's whiskey down," she said, smiling at Tom.

"Folks are gonna remember that for a long, long time," Ol' Man Barnes declared.

"I ain't gonna forgit it soon myself," Tom said, with feeling. As he pocketed his new bag of marbles and an extra nickel he asked, "Would you tell folks Pa's ready for some help on that schoolhouse-chapel down at the mission?"

Leaving the store, Tom headed toward the mill. But when he saw the group of men and boys sitting on the steps outside the building, away from the noise of the machinery, he forgot all about passing along Pa's message. Cat Johnson, his lanky body draped across several steps, was telling a tale.

Tom was soon listening as raptly as the others, watching Cat's expressive face and joining in the laughter. When Cat finished, he shifted his plug of tobacco to the other cheek and looked right at Tom. "Did your pa send you down here?" he asked.

Surprised, Tom nodded. "I'm supposed to spread the word that the foundation's laid an' he's ready for some carpentry help on that schoolhouse-chapel now."

"Wal, durn!" Cat said. "I thought maybe he sent you down here to learn how to tell a tale."

After the laughter died down, one of the men said, "You tell your pa I'll be there. I want my boys to learn to write their names so they don't have to sign a X like I do."

The murmur of agreement assured Tom that Pa would have all the help he needed.

A few nights later, Tom and Pa sat on the porch waiting for Andy to come up and swap tales. Tom was turning a block of wood over and over in his hands, trying to decide what he should carve, when he heard Andy's holler.

"Hey, Andy!" he called as the big man drew near the gate.

"Hey, Tom. Hey, June. How's everything with you?" Andy asked as he lowered himself into the rocking chair.

"Tolerable," Pa said, "Tolerable."

Tom was waiting patiently for the men to finish their ritual greetings so they could settle down to the story-telling when he heard the sound of hoofbeats.

"Wonder what's so dadburn important it couldn't wait till he saw me down at the buildin' site tomorrow mornin'?" Pa muttered when Preacher Taylor rode up.

Seeing the man's out-thrust jaw as he swung down from the saddle and strode toward the porch, Tom felt a little tingle of anticipation. This might be interesting!

"Somebody's been spreading lies about me, Higgins," the preacher said, ignoring Andy and Tom and not bothering with a greeting.

Pa shrugged. "I don't lie, so it couldn't of been me."

"It had to be one of the men down at the work site, and I want you to find out which one."

Pa sent a stream of tobacco juice off the porch. "Might help if I knew what he said."

The preacher's face reddened. "I'm not repeating it. It was insulting to me both as a minister of the gospel and as a man."

Tom grinned. "I know what he's talkin' about, Pa." He turned to the preacher and said, "You must mean that tale Cat Johnson told down at the mill about how you hit your thumb with the hammer an' then spent the rest of the afternoon apologizin' for what you said, an' then—"

"So it was Cat Johnson!" the preacher burst out. "How dare he? It's all lies! I never hit my thumb, much less allowed blasphemous words to pass my lips. And the part about the board wasn't true, either." He appealed to Pa. "You've been there all the time—you know it's all lies."

76

He ran his fingers through his hair, leaving it mussed.

Pa frowned and pursed his lips. "Far as I know, you ain't never hit your thumb, but what's this about a board?"

The preacher's hands clenched into fists and Tom could see the rise and fall of his chest as he began to breathe harder. He opened his mouth and shut it again.

Tom spoke for him. "Cat said the preacher picked up a real long board, an' when he turned 'round, the other end of it knocked everybody down. First it whacked you, Pa, an' pushed you into one of the Simpson brothers, an' then he fell an' knocked Cat over, an' then—"

"I can see it now! Like a row of dadburn dominoes." Pa threw back his head and laughed aloud.

"You know very well you saw nothing of the sort!" the preacher said, spluttering.

Still chuckling, Pa said, "You don't listen good, Preacher. I said 'I can see it now.' I didn't say I'd seen it then."

"What's that supposed to mean?"

"Cat Johnson wasn't lyin', Preacher. He was just tellin' a tale."

Tom nodded in agreement. "Fact is, he told it before they even started the carpentry work down there."

" 'Keep thy tongue from evil and thy lips from speaking guile,' " the preacher began, but Andy interrupted him.

"Cat Johnson's no liar, Charles—he's an entertainer. He gets his ideas from daily life and goes on from there, exaggerating and embellishing them. Anybody who hears that story will know it's just a tale."

"But he was making fun of me! And some boys taunted my daughter about it when she rode through the settlement this afternoon. I can't allow that."

Must have been Lonny and Harry, thought Tom. They probably asked Amy how her pa's thumb was and led her on from there.

"What you have to do, Charles," Andy said, "is find a way to turn that joke around."

When the preacher looked interested, Tom suggested, "How about havin' Miz Taylor bandage up your thumb, makin' it about the size of a egg. Then when you show up at the buildin' site an' the men ask what happened, you say, 'Didn't you hear about my accident with the hammer?' "

Andy puffed on his pipe. "Good idea. Good idea," he said, but to Tom's disappointment, Pa said nothing.

"That's it, then," said the preacher, standing up. "That's exactly what I'll do." Crossing the porch, he shook hands with each of them in turn before he strode jauntily across the yard and through the gate.

As the preacher rode out of sight, Pa asked accusingly, "How come you never told me Cat's story, boy?"

Tom pretended to be surprised. "I thought you knew. You was there when it all happened, wasn't you?"

Andy laughed, but Pa just gave a snort and sent a stream of tobacco juice off the porch. Disappointed that his father showed no appreciation for his quick-witted answer, Tom turned to Andy and asked, "What tale are you gonna tell tonight, seein' as you finally finished the one about the Greek kings?"

"There's a sequel to that tale—a story about what happened next, that is. It tells of the adventures Odysseus and his men had on their trip home."

"Tell that one, then," Tom said, opening his whittling knife. He'd decided to make another bird.

13

"What makes you think this here mash is ready to run, boy?" Pa challenged.

Peering into the barrel, Tom ticked off the reasons on his fingers as he recited confidently, "It ain't poppin' an' spittin' no more, the foam's gone from the top, an' the color's right."

Pa grunted his agreement. "Then git that there furnace fired up. When your mash reaches its peak, that's the time to run it—not some other time that might suit you better."

Hearing the note of warning in his father's voice, Tom hid his disappointment that they would miss this week's service at the brush tabernacle. He'd looked forward to hearing the preacher's Bible story and to catching up on all the news. As he lit the logs in the mud-chinked stone furnace he'd helped Pa build around the still pot, Tom ventured, "You think that preacher's gonna guess why we ain't there this mornin'?"

"He probably thinks he's keepin' me so busy down at that schoolhouse-chapel I don't have no time to make whiskey," Pa said scornfully. He checked the water-filled condensing barrel and the "worm" inside it. That coiled copper pipe was where the alcohol vapor rising from the mash heated in the still pot would cool into pure corn whiskey. Looking up, Pa gave Tom a conspiratorial grin and asked, "Wouldn't Petey Hudson just love to find this rig of ours?"

Suddenly, from behind them, a voice said, "I *have* found

it, Higgins," and the steely-eyed revenuer stepped forward.

It was a raid! Tom whirled around to flee and ran smack into Cory, the silent revenue agent who had come to the cabin with Hudson. Tom cried out as Cory twisted his arm behind his back and forced him to his knees. His heart pounded loudly in his ears and his breath came in rasping half sobs as he struggled to turn his head toward Pa.

To Tom's surprise, his father was leaning against one of the mash barrels, looking as relaxed as if he were talking to Lance Rigsby. Hudson and a third revenuer, their bodies tensed, stood nearby.

"Why, Petey," Pa drawled, "I thought I'd convinced you I ain't no moonshiner."

"You had," the revenuer said grimly, "but then one of your neighbors convinced me to take another look in your woods." With that, he signaled the third revenuer. The man filled a jar with fermented mash from one of the barrels—for evidence, Tom figured—and then set to work systematically destroying everything in sight.

Tom gasped when the ax split the hoops of the first barrel and the liquid splashed out in a great wave. Hardly believing what was happening, he watched the man splinter the other barrels and then set to work on the still itself. Tom winced as the man broke through the mud-daubed stone furnace to cut huge gashes in the copper pot and then chopped the worm into short sections.

At last Hudson said, "That's enough, Ralph," and with obvious reluctance, the man stopped.

Pa surveyed the ruined still impassively and said, "Wal, I guess I'll be seein' you in town Tuesday for court day, Petey."

Hudson didn't bother to reply. "Come on," he said to his men. "We'll take them in to the magistrate and then jail them."

Jail *them?* Tom's heart almost stopped. He'd never realized *he* might go to jail! He stumbled as Cory jerked him to his feet, and his stomach contracted with fear.

Pa spit a stream of tobacco juice so close to Ralph that the man jumped aside. "You can't take no minor child to jail, an' you know it," he scoffed.

Hardly breathing, Tom looked from Pa to P. D. Hudson, wondering if that was true—and fervently hoping it was.

The revenuers exchanged glances, and then Ralph said, "We might let him go if you agree to help us."

"Help you how?" Pa asked suspiciously.

"Tell us the name of another moonshiner, and I'll have Cory release the boy," Hudson said.

Tom gnawed at his lip. Some of the worst feuds in the hills began when a moonshiner found out a neighbor had turned him in.

Pa appeared to be thinking over the revenuer's offer. "Let me git this straight, Petey," he said. "If I give you the name of another moonshiner, you'll let the boy go. Is that right?" When Hudson nodded, Pa stepped forward and said, "Let's shake on that."

Hudson grasped Pa's outstretched hand, and Pa announced, "Hube Baker's been makin' moonshine for years."

"We already knew that," Cory said, breaking his customary silence.

Pa shrugged. "You never said it had to be some name you didn't know."

After a long pause, Hudson said, "He's right, Cory. Let

the boy loose." Glaring at Tom, he snapped, "Get on home now, before I change my mind."

Tom scrambled to his feet, and after a grateful look at Pa, he slipped away. As soon as the forest closed around him, he raced toward home. Once there, he just sat on the porch and waited, because he didn't know what else to do.

It seemed a long time before he saw the men coming through the orchard, walking single file, with Hudson in front of Pa and the other two revenuers behind him. As they passed the cabin, Tom lifted a hand in silent greeting, and Pa called, "Tell Preacher Taylor not to expect me down at the buildin' site no more."

For the rest of the morning, Tom sat numbly on the top step of the porch, feeling completely alone. He'd never imagined that something like this could happen, that revenuers could actually catch Pa. He'd taken for granted that Pa was too clever for that.

Tom was sure no carelessness of his had led the revenuers to the still. He figured they must have had to search every inch of the woods to find it. There was no telltale path because he and Pa always approached the still a different way. And following the stream wouldn't have been any help to the revenuers. It was impossible to spot the carefully concealed length of pipe that carried water to the wooden trough Pa had covered with a layer of decaying leaves. Tom scowled, remembering how hard Pa had worked to divert the water they needed for mixing the mash and cooling the vapor in the copper worm.

Finally, Tom dragged himself to his feet and set off for the mission to deliver Pa's message. His mind was in such turmoil that he was hardly aware of his surroundings, and he was surprised when he saw Princess running to meet him. He couldn't remember crossing the footlog, and here he was at the preacher's house already, he thought as he picked up the little dog. Wiggling in his arms, she managed to thoroughly lick his face as he hugged her, and Tom felt tears burning behind his eyes as he whispered, "I love you, too, Princess."

He looked up when Amy called to him, and his heart fell when he saw her sitting on the porch with her parents. He hadn't realized he might have to tell the preacher about Pa in front of Amy and her mother. Clutching Princess to him, Tom approached the house with faltering steps. "Pa won't—won't be able to work for you no more, Preacher Taylor," he stammered. "He's—he's—"

Mrs. Taylor led him to a chair. "Get him some water, Amy," she said, her voice full of concern.

"Now, Tom," Mrs. Taylor said after he had drained the glass, "Tell us what happened to your poor father. We knew something must be wrong when the two of you missed the service this morning."

Tom blurted out, "Pa's in jail."

"Thank God," Mrs. Taylor whispered.

Tom stared at her, and Amy explained, "She thought you meant he was dead. She's thanking God he's alive, not that he's in jail. Oh, Tom, how can you stand the disgrace?"

"Ain't no disgrace," Tom objected. "Just real hard luck."

Obviously controlling himself with difficulty, Preacher Taylor burst out, "It's worse than hard luck! How will my schoolhouse-chapel be finished without your father's leadership? And what's he doing in jail, anyway?"

Tom calmed himself by stroking Princess. "Revenuers caught him at his still this mornin' an' took him in," Tom said, careful not to let on that he'd been there, too.

"At his still?" The preacher's voice rose. "And was he planning to come to Sunday services straight from that evil work?"

Before Tom could answer, Mrs. Taylor quickly asked, "How long will your pa be in jail, Tom?"

"Depends on what the judge decides."

Still agitated, the preacher said, "I don't understand why Hube Baker's walking around free and they're keeping your father in jail till court day."

"That's Petey Hudson's doin'," Tom said, scowling. "Anyhow, court day's this Tuesday, and I'm goin' to the trial," he added importantly. He'd always wanted to go to Buckton, and now he had a reason to go there and nothing to stop him.

Mrs. Taylor gave Tom a searching look. "Have you ever been to town before, Tom?" she asked. "It's—well, it's a long way off."

He shook his head. "I ain't never been, but some folks go all the time." The distance hadn't kept the preacher from going there to send the sheriff after Hube Baker and again to send the revenuers up to the cabin, he thought bitterly.

Mrs. Taylor gave a quick nod and said, "Come on over to the clothing bureau then, Tom, and we'll find some town clothes for you." She led him over to what had once been Ollie Gentry's meat house. Inside, it still had a faint smoky scent, but otherwise it had been transformed. Shelves along one wall held shoes of all sizes and colors. Wooden boxes stacked high with folded sweaters lined the opposite wall, and in the back, shirts and dresses and pants hung from a wooden rod. Tom just stood and stared while Princess wiggled out of his arms to sniff around the small building.

"These should do," Mrs. Taylor said, taking down a pale blue shirt and a pair of dark blue pants. "I'll see if I can find a belt for you."

"Miz Taylor," Tom said, "I can't take these things."

"Why ever not?" she asked as she rummaged through a box.

" 'Cause I can't pay for 'em."

Mrs. Taylor straightened up and said, "You can work off the price by chopping wood."

Tom was just about to agree when Amy urged, "You'd better take the clothes, Tom. You certainly can't go to town wearing what you've got on."

He looked down at his faded shirt with a missing button and the overalls that ended too far up his legs. "I reckon I can go to town wearin' whatever I please," he said. Who did Amy think she was, telling him what he could and couldn't do?

Mrs. Taylor gave Amy a long look, and Amy hung her head and turned away. Tom watched her walk toward the house, dragging her feet through the grass. She didn't seem to notice Princess prancing along beside her.

"I, uh, have to go now, Miz Taylor," Tom said, edging out the door. Amy had no right to stand there in her charity dress and shoes, criticizing the clothes Pa paid for with hard-earned cash money, Tom thought resentfully as he strode along the weedy road. He turned down the path that led to the Widow Brown's cabin. She'd want to know about Pa, and it would do him good to talk to somebody who didn't look on it as a disgrace—or an inconvenience—that Pa was in jail.

A few minutes later, Mrs. Brown was listening intently to Tom's story. He was surprised how much better he felt after he'd told it all the way through—even the part about his trip to the mission. When he had finished, the two of them sat in silence for a few minutes, Mrs. Brown in her rocking chair and Tom perched on the porch rail.

At last Mrs. Brown roused herself and said, "Bring me my sewin' basket an' button jar off the mantel, Tom, an' shuck off your shirt so I can fix it. Then I'm gonna take my scissors to that head of hair I've been wantin' to git at for so long."

Tom threaded the needle for Mrs. Brown while she emptied the buttons into her lap and searched for the closest match. She pounced on one, then poured the others back into the jar and handed it to Tom, saying with mock severity, "Now don't let them folks in Buckton git close enough to see this button ain't got but two holes an' the rest have four, you hear?"

"I hear, Miz Brown," Tom said, grinning.

By the time he started for home, Tom was in better spirits, but back at the cabin the gloom he'd felt that morning returned. Instead of eating the biscuits and fried chicken Mrs. Brown had sent home with him, he stored them in the crock in the spring box and choked down the corn bread left from breakfast—corn bread Pa had baked before they went to the still.

Tom sat on the porch, brooding in the silence, for a long time before he went up to the loft and rummaged in his box until he found his slingshot. For a while he amused himself by seeing how far he could shoot the kernels of corn he found on the porch floor around the corn sheller, but he soon tired of that and sat on the step, dejected.

He'd been alone lots of times when Pa stayed at the still overnight to run his whiskey, but this was different. This time Pa was twelve miles away in a cell over in Buckton. The way the hours from Sunday evening till court day on Tuesday seemed to stretch endlessly ahead of him, Tom didn't think he could stand it if the judge sent Pa to jail for a year. He would have to move in with the Widow Brown, as she had urged that afternoon.

Tom's arm ached from Cory's rough treatment, and he rubbed it absently, remembering how he'd longed to go and live with Mrs. Brown during the lonely months after Ma left. Now he had the chance to do just that—and to share the loft with Andy, too. But all he wanted was to stay here with Pa.

When he heard Andy's holler some time later, Tom felt a little better. He'd forgotten that Andy had promised to stop by on his way back from the far side of the ridge, where he'd gone hoping to collect some stories.

"Hey, Tom!" Andy called as he neared the gate.

Running to meet him, Tom burst out, "Pa's in jail, Andy!"

"Jail!" Andy's eyebrows rose. "What happened?"

Tom swallowed hard and hoped his voice would be steady. "That Petey Hudson came back with his men an' caught us over at Pa's still."

"When was this?" Andy asked, lowering himself into the rocking chair and laying his notebook on the porch floor.

"Early this mornin'." As Tom described the raid, he felt a shadow of the terror that had filled him when Cory grabbed him. "Somebody told Petey Hudson to look 'round on Pa's land again," he said, finishing his story.

"But why's June in jail? I thought—"

"That Petey Hudson don't know how things are done 'round here!" Tom said heatedly. "He took Pa in to see the magistrate, an' he's keepin' him in jail till court day. That's this Tuesday."

Tom paused, breathing deeply to calm himself. "I still can't figure who could of told Petey Hudson. Unless," he said slowly, "unless maybe it was Eddie Jarvis gittin' back at Pa for makin' him pay Preacher Taylor for that pile of boards he'd set fire to."

"If I were you, I wouldn't mention that suspicion to anyone, especially your pa," Andy said meaningfully.

A chill passed through Tom as his eyes met Andy's. He hoped Eddie would keep his mouth shut and not gloat about what he'd done to King Higgins. If he really had done it, that is.

Andy rocked silently for a few minutes before he said, "There's room in Mrs. Brown's loft, if you want to come back with me."

Tom shook his head. "Not tonight. I might have to do that after court day, though," he said, resignation in his voice.

"Buckton's close enough that you'll be able to visit your pa," Andy said.

"If the judge gives him a year, they'll send him to the federal prison in Atlanta instead of keepin' him at the town jail," Tom said glumly. He'd heard that Atlanta was so far away it wasn't even in Virginia.

After a moment Andy said, "From what Mrs. Brown tells me, your pa has a lot of influence around here. I wonder what the results of his absence will be."

"For one thing, there probably won't be no school."

"I thought the building's almost finished."

"It is. But without Pa in charge, all them neighbors are gonna spend more time arguin' among theirselves than workin'. An' when the preacher comes over an' starts quotin' Bible verses at 'em, they're gonna remember how they didn't want no mission here in the first place. An' that'll be the end of it till Pa comes back." Tom sighed. "I'd really been countin' on learnin' to read an' write."

Andy sat looking across the cornfield for what seemed like a long time before he turned to Tom and said, "You told me about your pa's message for Preacher Taylor. What about the one for the men that were working on the building?"

"There wasn't none."

"Didn't he ask you to tell them he expected the work to be finished? And didn't he say who he wanted to be in charge?"

Tom's eyes grew wide, and his voice showed his excitement. "Lance Rigsby! He's the one Pa would of picked. An' instead of 'King Higgins *said*,' we tell 'em 'King Higgins *wants you to*.' That way it ain't no lie, 'cause Pa would of wanted it that way. Pa, he don't much like it when I lie," Tom added.

"Sounds like a good plan. I think your pa will approve, even if he never tells you so."

Tom said, "Guess I'll walk on down an' let Lance Rigsby know Pa wants him to be in charge of finishin' that buildin'. He can tell the others."

But Andy shook his head. "It would be better for the men to hear what King Higgins wants and then to tell Lance themselves. The Johnsons' place isn't far out of my way. I can give Cat the message if you don't think he'd object to hearing it from an outsider."

"Folks don't see you as a outsider no more—you ain't all that different from us, even if you do talk funny."

"Good," Andy said, bending over to pick up his notebook. "I'll be on my way then."

After Andy left, Tom felt very much alone. For want of anything better to do, he gathered a dozen or so small rocks. Aiming his slingshot at the top hinge of the gate, he fired one rock after another, hitting his target more often than he missed. He was gathering a second handful of rocks when he heard a holler, and much to his surprise, he saw Hube Baker coming up the trail.

"Hey, Mr. Baker," he called.

"Hey, Tom," the old man answered, leaving the gate open behind him as he walked up to the porch. He slumped down in the rocking chair and looked a little bit past Tom. "You doin' all right, boy?" he asked. "I seen 'em go by with June this mornin'."

Wondering now if it could have been Hube who told the revenuers about Pa's still, Tom said, "I'm doin' fine."

"You want to, you can come along to the courthouse with me on Tuesday," the man offered.

"I don't know yet if I'm goin'," Tom lied. Even if his shifty-eyed neighbor hadn't turned Pa in, Tom didn't want to have anything to do with him. Scowling, he thought of the bruises he'd seen on Emma Baker's face and arms.

"Now, jail ain't as bad as all that," Hube said, misinterpreting Tom's scowl. "Feller over in Ox Gore Holler was sent to Atlanta, an' he said it wasn't bad at all. They fed him three meals a day, an' he never had to lift a finger. They gave him a bran' new suit of clothes when his year was up, too."

"Sounds like you won't mind so much if the judge gives you a year," Tom said. Hube could use a suit of clothes— or even a clean pair of overalls, he thought.

Hube didn't answer, but a little smile played around the corners of his mouth as he pulled a flat bottle out of his pocket and unscrewed the lid. He acts like he knows something, Tom thought as he watched Hube throw back his head, take a long drink, and then smack his lips appreciatively.

Hube stood up and slipped the bottle back in his pocket. "Wal, lemme know if you're comin' to town with me on court day." Before he was out of sight, he brought the bottle out of his pocket again and drank deeply.

Tom frowned, thinking that poor Emma Baker would probably be bruised and sore again tomorrow, and suddenly he hoped Hube *would* be sent to jail for a year.

14

He should have set off earlier, Tom realized. He urged Ol' Sal along the rough, one-lane dirt road that linked the settlement at Nathan's Mill to Buckton. What if he missed Pa's trial? he thought as he passed the small farms and neatly planted orchards.

As he came into town an hour later, Tom reined in Ol' Sal and stared. The houses were so close together you could look out the windows of one and see right in the windows of the next! He started on, and the farther he went, the closer together the houses were, the more people he saw, and the more wagons—and automobiles—crowded the road. But to Tom's surprise, Ol' Sal didn't seem to mind the traffic.

Tom prodded her forward—he'd better not waste any time finding the courthouse. He figured it would be the largest building around, so he headed toward a stately white building on the right. But where were all the people? Mrs. Brown had told him folks from miles around came into Buckton on court day.

A man in a black suit came out of the building and paused when he saw Tom. "Is there something I can do for you?"

That must be the judge, Tom decided. "I've come for court day," he said.

"You're at the wrong place," the man told him. "This is the Methodist church. You'll find the courthouse if you go straight till you get to Main Street and then turn left."

At least he was headed in the right direction, Tom thought, keeping a tight hold on the reins, but how would he know when he came to Main Street? Suddenly there was a terrible screech, and an automobile stopped just inches away. A man leaned out the window and shouted, "What's the matter with you, kid? Don't you know what that deputy's hand signal means?"

Bewildered, Tom shook his head. He hadn't even noticed the uniformed man standing in the middle of the street.

"Don't you be fresh with me," the driver said, his voice shaking.

Tom didn't know what to say, or what to do, and he began to wish he hadn't come.

"Your first time in town, sonny?" someone asked.

Tom looked down and saw a silver-haired man with a shiny star pinned to his shirt. It was another of the sheriff's deputies. "Let me help you out of this mess," the deputy said, taking Ol' Sal's reins. "Now, where you headed for, young man?"

"The courthouse."

"Then we need to turn here," the deputy said, and when the other officer stopped the traffic, he led Ol' Sal across the intersection.

So this was Main Street, Tom thought, noticing with interest the hollow sound Ol' Sal's hooves made on its hard, black surface. His head was spinning as he looked from the farm wagons and automobiles that clogged the street to the buildings that lined the sidewalks. Buildings with windows that stretched all the way across the front and all kinds of goods laid out just inside them. Tools here, shoes there—even pies and crusty loaves of bread. Briefly, Tom shut his eyes to savor the aroma that wafted from the bakery door.

As the deputy led Ol' Sal across an unpaved side street, Tom craned his neck for a better look at a large open area where plows and harrows and pieces of farm equipment he didn't even recognize were arranged in rows. People were everywhere, and some of them seemed to be selling produce from their wagons.

"Is that a fair?" Tom asked, remembering how Lonny and Harry had lorded it over him with stories of last fall's county fair.

"That's the farmer's market," replied the deputy. A few minutes later he announced, "Well, here we are, son. You hurry on in, and I'll tie your horse for you."

Tom gaped at the courthouse, an imposing brick building with white columns and a domed roof. Its shady lawn and the wide stairs that led up to its massive wooden doors were dotted with groups of people, and Tom glimpsed Doc Mowbray and his brother Sol talking to some men from Ox Gore Hollow.

Inside, a man impatiently pointed to a sign when Tom asked where the trials were, and he followed the direction of the arrow under the words until he came to a pair of double doors. He hesitated, then squared his shoulders and opened them.

People standing in the back of the courtroom blocked his way, but he squeezed past them, ignoring the grumbles and complaints as he worked his way forward. Finally, he stood behind the last row of benches. At the front of the huge room he saw a nervous-looking man who sat facing the crowd and two other men in city clothes who were talking quietly with the judge. Awed, Tom gazed around him, thinking he'd never seen anything so grand— or seen so many people in one place before. He jumped when the judge brought down his gavel and said, "Case dismissed."

For a moment, the man facing the crowd looked surprised, but when a cheer went up from one side of the courtroom he grinned widely, shook hands with both of the men who'd been talking to the judge, and headed for the door. The judge banged his gavel and called out, "Order in the court!" as a group of people left their seats to follow the man down the aisle and some men who had been standing along the wall made their way toward the vacant seats.

"Junior Higgins."

Tom snapped to attention, and his eyes searched the room until he saw his father making his way to the chair in the front.

"Do you swear to tell the truth, the whole truth, and nothing but the truth, so help you God?" a man asked, handing Pa a Bible.

"I do." His voice wasn't loud, but it was easily heard.

The judge peered over his spectacles at Pa and said, "You've been charged with operating a still in violation of the laws of this land. How do you plead?"

"I ain't gonna plead with you, Judge," Pa said. "I know I broke the law, an' I'm gonna take my punishment like a man."

Tom frowned as someone in the audience tittered, and he glanced up irritably as a young man with a notebook squeezed his way in to stand beside him.

"Are you admitting you're guilty as charged?"

"I'm admittin' I was runnin' a still," Pa said, "but I ain't admittin' I'm guilty. All I've done is earn a livin' for myself an' my boy by makin' an' sellin' somethin' folks want to buy."

A murmur rippled through the room, and people nodded their heads. The judge banged his gavel again. "Mr. Higgins," he said sternly, "don't you understand that you must obey this nation's laws whether you agree with them or not?"

"I understand that if I'm caught breakin' the law, I'll be brought to court an' punished for it."

Tom's heart swelled with pride. He was glad the judge couldn't make Pa say he'd done wrong. Tom hoped he'd grow up to be just like his pa.

The young man standing beside Tom scribbled in his

notebook, and the judge took off his glasses and began to polish them with a large white handkerchief. After he'd put them back on, he asked, "Are you saying that if I send you to jail, you'll just go back to making corn liquor again as soon as you get out?"

"*You're* the one sayin' that," Pa answered.

At the burst of laughter, the judge banged his gavel and glared at the audience. Then he turned back to Pa and said, "But you aren't denying it, are you?"

"I swore to tell the truth, Judge."

When the crowd quieted down, the judge asked, "Mr. Higgins, are you a man of your word?"

"I am," Pa said proudly.

"In that case, I'll suspend your sentence if you promise me you'll never make corn liquor again."

Tom held his breath. What would Pa say to that? Making whiskey was more than Pa's livelihood—it was his life.

"You have my word," Pa said, raising his right hand. "I'll never make corn likker again as long as I live."

The courtroom erupted into applause, and Tom heard himself cheering as Pa walked down the aisle a free man. The sound of the judge's gavel was lost in the commotion, and the young man with the notebook turned to Tom and asked, "Do you know who that man is?"

"He's my pa," Tom said over his shoulder as he struggled through the crowd. Beneath his elation that Pa was free, questions tumbled through his mind. How would Pa pay his land tax now? Would he regret that he'd bargained a year of freedom for giving up stilling for the rest of his life? *Had Pa done that for him?*

Pa was halfway down the sidewalk by the time Tom

caught up, and the young man with the notebook was right behind him.

"Excuse me, sir," the man said, tapping Pa's shoulder. "I'd like to talk to you for a minute." Pa looked him up and down, from the top of his slicked-back hair to his brown and white shoes, until a blush began to creep up the young man's face. "I'm from the county newspaper," he explained. "I'd like to do a story on you."

"Do what you please," Pa said, turning away. "Come on, boy. We've got a long way to go."

The reporter hurried to get in front of them. Walking backward, he said, "What I mean is, I'd like to ask you some questions about your trial. Are you really going to stop making corn liquor?"

Pa grabbed the reporter's bow tie, jerked him close, and asked, "You hard of hearin', mister? You ain't? Then your question's downright insultin'! You heard me tell that judge I'm a man of my word, an' you heard me tell him I'd never make corn likker again." He glared at the young man a moment more before he shoved him away.

Pa strode off, leaving Tom to follow on Ol' Sal. As he untied the horse Tom looked back and saw the shaken young reporter running his finger around the inside of his collar and staring after Pa.

Ol' Sal walked along placidly, and Tom watched the people passing on the sidewalk and going in and out of the stores. They reminded him of ants streaming to and from their nest. Away from Main Street, he looked at the houses and wondered what it would be like to live where strangers went past all day long.

It wasn't until they were out of town, starting up the narrow dirt road toward the settlement, that Pa spoke.

"Guess I'd better plan on gettin' things started again down at that schoolhouse-chapel. Bet them fellers was on their way home before noon yesterday."

Tom heard a hint of satisfaction in Pa's voice and wondered if he and Andy had made a terrible mistake. Thinking fast, he said, "They wouldn't of dared."

"Just what do you mean by that?" Pa demanded.

"Soon as they heard King Higgins wanted 'em to finish the job an' wanted Lance Rigsby in charge, they knew they'd better do what was expected of 'em."

For once Pa was speechless, and Tom took advantage of that to add, "Andy asked Cat Johnson to pass on that message after I gave your other message to the preacher."

Tom waited tensely until Pa said, "Good thing you reminded me about that, boy. I'd clean forgot."

Pa wasn't mad at him! Tom was wishing it had been his own idea instead of Andy's when he heard a shout. He looked back and saw Hube Baker riding toward them, a comical sight on his old mule. Hube must have promised not to make corn liquor anymore, too, Tom thought. He wondered why the judge couldn't tell Hube wasn't the kind of man who kept his word.

"Guess I'll be gittin' a lot of new customers now that you won't be stillin' no more," Hube said, stopping beside them and grinning as he looked just past Pa.

"Sounds like you're fixin' to break your word to the judge," Pa said disapprovingly, ignoring the fact that the old man had to sell his whiskey in Buckton because no one in the hills would drink it.

Hube grinned even wider. "I didn't have to make him no promise. You're lookin' at a innocent man."

"Innocent!" Pa and Tom exclaimed together. And then

Pa said, "I thought the sheriff caught you carryin' your whiskey home."

" 'Deed he did," Hube chortled. " 'Deed he did."

Tom looked at Hube with distaste. "Then how come the judge thought you was innocent?" he asked bluntly.

"Oh, he didn't think I was innocent," Hube said. "He knew I was guilty, all right, but he couldn't do nothin' about it, 'cause there weren't no evidence against me."

Pa's face showed his disbelief. "You don't mean to tell me the sheriff didn't take no jar of whiskey to hold for evidence."

Hube gave a cackling laugh. " 'Course he did! But he didn't hold it long, 'cause that fat little deputy is a customer of mine, an' he made sure that there evidence plumb disappeared. He likes havin' enough whiskey for him an' all his friends delivered right to his door, don't you see." Still chuckling, Hube dug his heels into his mule and left Tom and Pa staring after him.

15

That evening Tom sat on the porch, tired but content, watching a jaybird take shape under his knife.

"Wal, boy," Pa said, breaking the silence, "we better start thinkin' about settin' up a new still."

Tom stared at his father. "But you just promised that judge you'd stop makin' moonshine!"

"You don't listen good," Pa said. "I promised I'd stop making corn likker, but I never said I wouldn't make no fruit brandy."

Tom laughed, realizing he should have known Pa would never give up stilling so easily. The preacher couldn't stop June Higgins from making moonshine, and the revenuers couldn't, either.

Using the point of his knife to carve out a small ring of wood, Tom left a raised circle for his jaybird's eye and then carefully rounded the edges. Cranking the cider mill to grind the apples for brandy was hard work, he thought, and it took a long time for the apple pomace to ferment. But making peach brandy was easier and quicker.

The sound of hoofbeats interrupted Tom's thoughts, and he looked up to see Preacher Taylor approaching. Looping the reins over the gatepost, he walked to the porch, a pleased smile on his face. "I'm proud of you, Brother Higgins," he said. "Mighty proud."

Pa looked at him quizzically. "Don't rightly know what you're talkin' about, Preacher Taylor," he said.

"I was afraid you were lost, but I just heard the good news when I rode through the settlement."

Pa frowned and asked, "How could I be lost when I've lived here all my life?"

Tom hid a grin, wondering how Pa could string the preacher along time after time without the man ever catching on.

"I meant lost at the Judgment Day," Preacher Taylor explained, brushing off the porch step before he sat down.

"We don't call it Judgment Day 'round here, Preacher," Pa said. "We say 'court day.' An' I've been to town more 'n once, you know."

Trying again, the preacher said, "I came up here to say how glad I am that you've seen the error of your ways and given up making liquor, Brother Higgins. My prayers have been answered."

Tom waited expectantly to hear what Pa would say. He had a feeling the cat-and-mouse game was over.

"You listen here," Pa said harshly, making one of the lightning-quick changes of disposition Tom was never quite prepared for. "My only error was gittin' caught. An' I gave up makin' likker in answer to the judge's question, Preacher, not in answer to no prayer of yours."

Preacher Taylor's jaw tightened. "You're as much as telling me my mission makes no difference in the lives of people in these hills. If that's true, I'm a failure." Looking skyward, he quoted, " 'Why art thou cast down, O my soul? And why art thou disquieted within me?' "

"The mission school's gonna make a difference in our lives, an' Miz Taylor's clothing bureau will, too," Tom said quickly. He didn't want to lose his chance to learn to read because Pa's words made the preacher so discouraged that he went back to the city.

"You're right, Tom," the preacher said, standing up. "I mustn't expect too much too soon." Then he turned to Pa and said stiffly, "I'll see you at the building site in the morning, Higgins."

In the waning light, Tom watched Preacher Taylor walk toward the gate and hoped he never found out Pa had only given up making corn whiskey.

As he drew near Harry's cabin two days later, Tom told himself that if any revenuers were watching, they would think he was coming to visit his friend and not suspect he was ordering mash barrels from Harry's father. "Hoo-hoo!" he hollered. "Hoo-hoo!"

Harry came around the corner of the cabin and called, "C'mon back!"

Tom opened the gate and went around the cabin, ignoring the two nondescript dogs sniffing at his ankles. He stood quietly, watching Harry pound a barrel head into place under his father's supervision. It must be nice to be able to do your work right out in plain sight, Tom thought.

Finally, Harry straightened up and said, "I gotta help Pa all day. We got a big order from—"

"Shut your mouth, boy," his father said, giving him a shove.

Another moonshiner, Tom realized, and one who was doing a powerful lot of stilling. He wondered who it could be but was glad the cooper protected his customers even if Harry didn't have the sense to. "Actually, I've come to order barrels for Pa, Mr. Perkins," Tom said. "Soon as you can have 'em ready, he needs—"

"I thought he promised the judge he wasn't gonna make no more whiskey," Harry interrupted.

The words were hardly out of Harry's mouth when his father boxed his ears. "I thought I told you to shut your mouth!"

"Pa ain't gonna make whiskey. He's makin' fruit brandy from now on." Tom was glad he could set the record straight so folks would know Pa wasn't breaking his word to the judge. Harry would make sure everyone heard all about it soon enough.

Harry's father chuckled. "Good for him," he said. "I don't drink, but I don't like to see the gov'ment interferin' with a man's livelihood. Your pa can have some of those," he added, gesturing toward a shed where barrels were lined up and stacked two deep. "Tell him he can give me a day's help at harvest time in return."

"If your pa's settin' up another still, I guess you ain't gonna have much time to yourself for a while, neither," Harry said, his eyes straying to the bundles of barrel staves stacked nearby, ready to be assembled.

"Guess not. Might not see you till school starts."

But Harry's father said, "Harry ain't goin' to that school. He's gonna stay here an' help me make barrels for folks to ship their apples out in. That boy may not know when to keep his mouth shut, but he's a good worker."

"School's for young'ns," Harry added scornfully, but Tom thought he saw a faint blush of pleasure color his friend's cheeks at the words *he's a good worker*.

"Wal, I'm goin'," Tom said "so if you ever need me to read you somethin', just ask." As he pushed aside the dogs so he could open the gate, Tom wasn't sure whether to envy Harry his father's praise or to pity him because he'd never learn to read.

Walking through the settlement, he decided to stop at the Rigsbys' and find out whether Lonny planned on going to school. Tom hollered as he walked down the lane, and Mrs. Rigsby came outside and called, "Lonny ain't here, but come on in an' try my blackberry jam on a piece of fresh-baked bread." Tom didn't need a second invitation, and when he started home, he was carrying a jar of jam.

When he reached the cabin, Pa said, "About time you showed up. I'm gonna make the new worm—got everything ready while you was gone."

"Can I help?" Tom asked. He remembered the time Pa made a worm for a man from the other side of the ridge.

He'd packed a long copper pipe with sand so that it wouldn't fold shut on itself, and then he'd twisted it around and around a stump until it looked like a giant bedspring.

" 'Course you can help," Pa said, eyeing the jar Tom had set on the porch. "Why else would I of waited till you was through visitin' all your friends—an' a kitchen or two on your way home? Come on, now."

Behind the cabin, Pa picked up the copper pipe Ol' Man Barnes had brought him from the hardware store in town. "Higgins men have always taught their sons the craft of stillin' and passed down their formulas for corn whiskey and fruit brandy," he said. "Makin' the best whiskey an' brandy in all these hills is your birthright, boy. It's somethin' I'm proud to teach to you, and someday you'll be proud to teach it to your son."

Tom didn't know what to say. Pa had never talked to him like this before, like he really cared.

"Yessiree, you're carryin' on a family tradition that dates back four or five generations," Pa continued, talking as they worked. "I never promised I wouldn't teach nobody how to make corn likker, by gum."

Later, when they stepped back to admire the finished worm, Pa said, "Now come on down to that ol' abandoned homesite where I'm settin' up the rig, an' I'll show you where to start buildin' the furnace."

Finding his voice, Tom asked, "I'm gonna build the furnace? By myself?"

"Might as well do somethin' to earn your keep," Pa said. "Besides, I gotta get down to that schoolhouse-chapel for a while. Lance Rigsby's buildin' the pulpit an' showin' the men how to make them benches, but I want to see how they're gettin' along."

Lonny must be over there helping with the benches, Tom thought.

"Don't you forget how I showed you to make the flue, 'cause if you make a furnace that don't draw good, you're gonna tear it down an' build it up right."

Tom refused to let Pa spoil his pride in being allowed to build the furnace around the still pot they'd patched the night before. But he couldn't help feeling a little envious of Lonny, working with the men at the building site. He wished stilling weren't such lonely work.

16

Tom wiped his sweating brow, leaving a streak of mud on his face. The sun beat down on his back as he gave the oozing red clay one last stir with his shovel and began to scoop it into the buckets. At least he wouldn't have to carry those buckets, he thought, struggling to lift them onto the heavy wooden land sled he'd found near the ruin of the old homesite's barn. Then he picked up the rope, and leaning into it with all his weight, he pulled the loaded "slide" toward the spring, where he would build the furnace.

He thought enviously of Pa supervising the finishing touches on the schoolhouse-chapel while he labored here alone. Then, guiltily, Tom remembered the nights he'd slept while Pa had worked, making trip after trip, lugging barrels and carrying down the copper still pot they'd patched. Tom gritted his teeth and resolved to work without complaining, the way Pa did.

Dragging the buckets of mud off the slide and around the uprooted pine that shielded the still from the clearing, Tom surveyed the rocks he'd hauled earlier. As he studied the still pot with its crazy quilt of patches, measuring it with his eyes, little tingles of excitement ran up and down his spine at the idea of building the furnace by himself. This was his chance to make Pa proud of him.

First, Tom scratched a circle in the dirt and checked to make sure it was a few inches larger than the widest part of the copper pot. Next, he shoveled out a thick layer of the gooey mud, spreading it along the outside of the circle he'd drawn. Then, choosing the flattest of the rocks, he set to work, pressing them solidly into the mud and carefully filling the spaces between them with mud, too. He knew the importance of building the furnace carefully so that no heat could escape between the rocks.

At the last minute, Tom remembered to leave an opening in front so they could fuel the furnace. Pa wouldn't have let him forget it for the rest of his life if he'd built a furnace and hadn't left a place to feed in the logs.

A breeze stirred the humid air as Tom started toward the jumble of rocks that had once been the foundation of a cabin, and glancing up, he saw billowing white clouds forming. "Thunderheads," he muttered. The sunlight had a brassy look, and as Tom watched, the clouds were becoming edged with gray. He cupped his hands to his ears and listened. Sure enough, he could hear a faint rumbling in the distance. He hated the thought of working in the rain, but if he quit, Pa would probably chide him and say it was all part of being a moonshiner.

Keeping watch for snakes, Tom gathered rocks to build the next layers of the furnace. Then, wearily, he pulled the slide toward the spring. By the time he'd unloaded it, his back was sore, and his fingers were stiffening up from the punishment his hands had taken.

Tom filled his buckets at the spring and wrestled them onto the slide, splashing himself in the process. Then, trying to ignore his fatigue, he set off to mix another batch of mud. He hadn't realized how much mortar the job would take. Or that the sun would have baked the red-clay soil so hard that he could barely dig it until it had been thoroughly soaked. Tom tried to remember why he had been so pleased with being allowed to build the furnace by himself.

He had loaded the slide with his buckets of mud and was pulling it back to the furnace when a gruff voice just behind him froze him in his tracks.

"What you doin' here, boy? This ain't your land."

Tom grabbed the shovel and used both hands to swing it around in a wide arc, sending it crashing into the man's leg. With a muffled oath, the man went down, and Tom lit off into the woods, ignoring the branches slapping at him and the roots grabbing at his feet. Minutes later he stopped, gasping for breath. He was safe now, he figured. No revenuer would bother to chase a boy through the woods—he'd wait to catch the man who was in charge of the still. To catch Pa!

"I gotta warn him," Tom said, his voice sounding loud in the silent woods. He skirted a tangle of greenbrier and then cut diagonally downhill through the open woods until he came out on the path. Tom hesitated when he saw a man limping toward him, and then he realized it was Pa. "Pa! What happened?"

"You know durn well what happened, boy," Pa growled, resting his weight on a stout stick.

Tom stared at him, mouth open. And then he saw the broad smear of red clay on the leg of Pa's overalls. He swallowed hard. "I—I didn't know it was you, Pa. Honest I didn't! I thought it was a revenuer. I guess I shouldn't have swung that shovel till I made sure. That was a big mistake."

"I'm the one that made the mistake," Pa admitted, "jokin' you like that. Now come along home before this storm breaks. We stopped work early down at the mission 'cause it looked so threatenin'."

An ominous rumbling made Tom aware of how still the air was and how dark the woods had become. "Guess I'll find me a platform stone to hold up the still pot an' finish that furnace t'morrer," he said, waiting hopefully for Pa to comment on the good job he'd done so far.

"You better," Pa said. "It ain't anywheres near half done yet."

17

"Too bad you ain't makin' whiskey no more, June," Hube Baker said slyly as he eased himself into the rocking chair on the porch the next evening. "If you was, you could be a rich man."

"That so, Hube?" Pa's hands were busy with the chair

seat he was weaving from white oak splits, and he didn't bother to look up.

" 'Deed it is, June. 'Deed it is."

Tom watched Hube slouch deeper into the chair, wondering how long it would be before the wiry little man told them the news he was bursting with.

Hube pulled a bottle from his pocket and took a long drink. Wiping his mouth on his sleeve, he put the bottle away and said, "Just you wait an' see, June. A lot of folks 'round here are gonna be gettin' rich."

"That so, Hube?" Pa asked.

"That's so, June." Hube waited until it was obvious Pa wasn't going to ask him more, and then he said, "A stranger down at the store said he'd buy all the whiskey we could make. An' he said he'd tell us how to speed up makin' it. Said the offer's good for all my friends, so if you want, I might could ask if he buys fruit brandy."

Tom glanced at Pa, wondering how he liked being included as a friend of Hube's. Pa was frowning. "Did I hear you say you was gonna speed up makin' your whiskey? It won't be half as good if you do that," he objected.

"But I'll be makin' more 'n twice as much, you see," Hube said. "Besides, I'm gonna age that whiskey two years in three days, like the man told me to."

"How can you do that?" Tom asked, forgetting that he didn't want anything to do with Hube Baker.

Hube turned and looked just past Tom's left ear. "I char me some oak chips and put 'em in the whiskey and it turns a golden-brown color. Just like it was aged in oak barrels, the man said." Hube paused to let them digest that before he added, "An' he told me how to speed up the stillin'." Leaning forward he said, "Bet you didn't know addin' a bit of potash an' some ground-up taters will speed things up an' git you more whiskey, too. An' addin' lye gives a sharper flavor. What do you think of that, June?"

Pa's hands gripped the edges of the unfinished chair seat. "I think it's a crime, what you're fixin' to do. Ain't you got no pride?"

Hube shrugged. "I don't see nothin' wrong with bein' modern. Like the man said, why should we still be makin' whiskey the same way our grandpappies did?"

" 'Cause it's a family tradition," Tom said.

Pa began weaving the white oak splits again. " 'Course, if a man never had no reputation to uphold, I can see why he might not care about the quality of his product," he said bluntly.

Tom glanced over at Hube, but the man didn't seem to realize he'd been insulted. "Wal," he said, getting to his feet, "lemme know if you change your mind, an' I'll find out if that feller buys fruit brandy."

Neither Tom nor Pa spoke until long after Hube was out of sight. When Tom saw that the taut set of Pa's jaw had finally relaxed, he asked, "Who do you think that man is, the one buyin' all Hube's whiskey?"

"A bootlegger." Pa spit a stream of tobacco juice off the porch. "One of them that buys whiskey from the stillers an' drives it to the city to sell." Pa tacked the end of the last white oak split to the chair frame and sat back to admire his handiwork.

Tom admired it, too, proud that Pa had made the chair Mrs. Taylor would use when school started on Monday. Monday! Now that the day he'd been waiting for was so near, Tom felt a little nervous. He welcomed the sound of Andy's holler—a good story would keep him from worrying about school.

"I met Hube Baker on the path," Andy remarked after the greetings were over.

Pa snorted. "He's been up here braggin' on how he's gonna make twice as much whiskey in half the time an' sell it all to some bootlegger," he said in disgust.

"Ah, a bootlegger. That explains the automobile tracks down at the settlement," Andy said thoughtfully. Then he, too, inspected the new chair. "If you make another one of these, I'd like to watch and take some notes," he said.

"You mean you ain't never seen nobody make a chair before?" Tom asked in surprise. "Not in your whole life?"

Andy shook his head. "In the city, folks buy most of the things they need instead of making them." He reached for the half-full jar Pa offered him.

"Swallers real smooth, don't it?" Pa asked when Andy handed back the jar. "Better enjoy good whiskey while you can, before this Pro'bition ruins it."

"We both know there's no way that law can be enforced, June."

"That ain't what I mean," Pa said. "I know Pro'bition ain't gonna *stop* moonshinin', but it's gonna *ruin* it, sure as we're sittin' here on this porch."

Tom had never heard his father talk like this before. "Ruin it, Pa? How?"

"Wasn't you listenin' when Hube talked about addin' potash an' ground-up taters an' even lye to his mash?"

"Yeah, but that's just ol' Hube, ain't it?" Tom couldn't imagine anybody else even thinking of doing what Hube was planning. Potatoes couldn't hurt anybody, but lye sure could. Women used potash and lye when they made soap!

Pa snorted. "Just Hube an' a lot of others who care more about makin' money than they do about makin' good whiskey."

Andy finished lighting his pipe and leaned back in the rocking chair. "You may be right, June," he said thoughtfully. "A lot of pop-skull liquor's being sold in the cities nowadays."

Pop-skull likker. The word itself almost made Tom's head hurt. "But nobody'd ever buy a second time from any moonshiner who made pop-skull likker, would they, Andy?"

"The customers have no idea who made the whiskey they buy, and even if the bootleggers knew, they wouldn't care. They're in it for the money."

"What do they buy with all that money, Andy?" Tom asked.

"Jewels and furs for their women. Fancy clothes. Faster automobiles so they can make more trips and get more money to buy things they don't need." Andy sounded sad and weary.

Tom couldn't imagine why anyone would risk going to jail to make money to buy things they didn't need. Soon as Pa sold Ol' Man Barnes enough moonshine to pay his due bills at the store and get cash money for his land tax, he'd do one more run to last him and Mrs. Brown the winter. Then he'd be through stilling for the year. He might have been almost through by now, Tom thought, if it hadn't been for Amy and the revenuers.

The three of them sat silently, each lost in his own thoughts, until Andy roused himself and said, "Mrs.

Brown was wondering if you had any 'buttermilk' left, June. Her rheumatism's acting up again, and she needs some to make the remedy that eases it."

"This here's my last jar, but I'll fill up your flask to last her till we run that peach brandy," Pa said. "With folks' peaches comin' in now an' one kind of apple or another ripenin' after that, we're gonna be right busy."

Tom hoped they wouldn't be so busy that Pa would change his mind about letting him go to the mission school.

18

Sunlight poured through the windows of the schoolhouse-chapel and fell on the floor in distorted golden rectangles. It was so bright and airy that Tom could almost imagine he was outdoors. And even with nearly everyone from Bad Camp Hollow and Nathan's Mill and Ox Gore Hollow there, it didn't seem crowded. Tom's eyes roved around the building, marveling at the pale color of the walls and floor. What a contrast to his low-ceilinged cabin with its logs stained dark by time and smoke.

Tom suddenly realized that everyone was standing. He scrambled to his feet and joined in the opening hymn, as Mrs. Taylor led the singing. Amy must be right proud of her ma, he thought, watching the trim, dark-haired little woman's hands mark the beat.

Sitting on the bench again, Tom waited expectantly, hoping this morning's Bible story would be as good as the ones Preacher Taylor had told at the brush tabernacle. But to Tom's disappointment, all the preacher did was talk about how much it meant to him to have the schoolhouse-chapel finished. He even talked about how Pa and the other men had built it, something everyone already knew. Tom stopped listening and began to watch a spider crawl along the floor.

It seemed as though hours had dragged by when he sensed a change in the mood of the congregation. Paying attention now, Tom heard the preacher say, " . . . so I ask God to forgive the misguided sinners who work at their stills. And I ask those men to follow the example of June Higgins, who has stopped degrading our community by making moonshine liquor."

An undercurrent of tension swept through the room, and Tom's heart pounded so hard that he was surprised the front of his shirt wasn't bouncing up and down for everyone to see. He stared straight ahead, not daring to look at either the preacher or Pa. Then, as Tom had known he would, Pa rose slowly to his feet. The preacher's words died away, and he asked hesitantly, "Do you, uh, have something to say, Brother Higgins?"

"I want to set somethin' straight," Pa said. "I ain't stopped degradin' this community, 'cause I never was degradin' it in the first place. An' I didn't see to it you got this here schoolhouse-chapel built to have you stand up there an' insult me in front of all my neighbors. Don't you forgit that again, Preacher."

There was a murmur of agreement and a nodding of heads in the congregation as Pa sat down again. The preacher's face grew pale, and he opened his mouth and closed it again, swallowing hard. Watching him, Tom scarcely breathed. Then something blue caught his eye, and he saw Mrs. Taylor standing in front of the congregation.

"We're expecting all the children and young people here for school tomorrow morning," she said. "Meanwhile, we'll close the service with 'Amazing Grace.' "

She gave the pitch, and the people joined in the song. Pa's voice was deep and steady, but Tom was sure his would waver, so he just stood and listened. The preacher wasn't singing, either—his jaws were tightly clenched.

Outside a few minutes later, the women and older girls gathered around Mrs. Taylor, and the men talked in groups of three or four. The smaller children ran and shouted, releasing pent-up energy after sitting quietly through the long service.

"Ma says for you an' Tom to come on home and take dinner with us," Lonny Rigsby said, addressing Pa.

"Tell her that would be mighty nice," Pa replied.

Lonny left to deliver Pa's message, and Tom said, "One of the best things about these Sunday services is bein' invited home for dinner with somebody every week."

"Molly Rigsby's cookin' oughta help us forgit that poor excuse for a sermon," Pa agreed as he left to join a group of men.

When Lonny came back, Tom asked, "How come you ain't plannin' on bein' here for school t'morrer?"

The other boy shrugged. "Ma wanted me to come, but I don't see no reason to learn to read. I ain't got no books."

"Pa's Bible ought to be enough readin' to last me awhile," Tom said, thinking of the thick, black book gathering dust on the mantel. He hadn't seen Pa touch it since the day he'd slipped Ma's note between its pages.

"After what happened a few minutes ago, it's hard to believe your father has a Bible," Amy said as she joined them. "He ruined the service, getting up like that," she said accusingly. "Father wasn't anywhere near finished with his sermon."

Before Tom could answer, Lonny said, "He'd talked long 'nough for me—them benches is hard."

Amy looked at him scornfully. "Some of us are more concerned about our souls than our seats," she said.

"My soles are tough from goin' barefoot, but I'd sure hate to have to stand on 'em through one of them long sermons," Lonny said, winking at Tom.

Amy opened her mouth to reply but apparently thought better of it. Tom's eyes followed her as she stalked away. He was glad Lonny had drawn Amy's attention away from him and hoped she'd have forgotten her displeasure by the next time he stopped at the mission to play with Princess.

"C'mon, Tom, let's go," Lonny said, nudging him.

The boys headed for the Rigsbys' wagon and piled into the back with Lonny's older brothers and sisters. Mrs. Rigsby joined them, boosted in by her husband and Pa before they climbed onto the wagon seat. Molly Rigsby, a fat, jolly woman, embarrassed Tom by circling her fingers around his wrist and saying, "You better come home with us more often so's I can put some meat on your bones, child!"

As they rolled toward the settlement, Tom had to admit there were advantages to living where it wasn't steep and rocky, where there was a wagon road instead of just footpaths. But he knew Pa would never trade the privacy and freedom of living high on the mountain for the convenience of level fields and a road—and neither would he.

At the Rigsbys' place, the boys set a tin can on the pasture fence and took turns trying to knock it off with Lonny's slingshot. Tom was three hits ahead when the dinner bell rang, and he was sure he'd have done even better with his own slingshot instead of one he wasn't used to.

The two boys raced to the table, and Tom heaped his plate with cabbage slaw and mashed potatoes and green beans cooked with salt pork. Then he spread butter on bread still warm from the oven while he waited for Lonny to pass him the fried chicken. Lance Rigsby and his other sons were already bent over their plates, as though a meal like this was the most ordinary thing in the world, and Tom realized that for them, it was. He helped himself to a chicken leg and began to eat.

After dinner, Tom would have been content to sit in the shade with Lonny's older brothers and the men, but Lonny started down the lane toward the settlement, motioning for Tom to follow. "Where we goin'?" he asked as they walked. It was too hot to move so fast after a big meal.

"Down to the mill to do some spyin'. Hurry up, or we'll be too late."

Spying? What was there to spy on down at the mill, especially on a Sunday? Tom was even more mystified when Lonny ducked under the plank steps and lay flat on his stomach so he could peer out between them and not be seen. But Tom did the same, and it wasn't long before he heard the sound of a motor.

"There he is," Lonny whispered as an automobile drove up and lurched to a stop in front of the store. After the dust had settled, a slim, well-dressed young man got out and carefully wiped the hood with his handkerchief before he leaned against it. "That's the bootlegger," Lonny whispered.

In broad daylight? Tom was speechless.

Lonny poked him and hissed, "An' look, here she comes, right on time."

Tom turned his head and saw the storekeeper's pretty granddaughter, Mary Barnes, hurry around the corner of the building. To his amazement, the bootlegger started toward her, his arms outstretched, and he held her close and kissed her when they met.

"Now he's gonna take her drivin'," Lonny whispered as the couple walked to the car, arms around each other. "An' he took her to the ice-cream parlor in Buckton two nights last week."

Probably loaded up with jars of whiskey after he brought her home, Tom thought. He sat up as they drove off, leaving a cloud of dust hanging in the air. "Does Ol' Man Barnes know about this?" he asked.

"Miz Barnes told Ma he can't do nothin' about it," Lonny said, brushing off his clothes. "Mary says she'll run off with that feller if they try to stop her from seein' him."

Pa would never have let a girl of his go riding with a bootlegger, Tom thought as he and Lonny walked back to the Rigsby place.

For the rest of the visit, Tom mulled over what he had seen from his spot beneath the mill steps. And on the way home that evening, he told Pa that Mary Barnes was keeping company with a bootlegger against her grandparents' wishes.

Pa muttered a curse. "That man's usin' her as cover so the sheriff an' Petey Hudson won't suspect the real reason he comes drivin' in an' out of the holler so often," he said.

Any revenuer ought to be smart enough to see through that, Tom thought, but he wasn't about to say so. And then Pa burst out, "I wonder how them dadburn do-gooders that got us that Pro'bition law would like it if bootleggers was ruinin' *their* daughters?"

The bootlegger wouldn't be coming here if nobody was selling him whiskey, and nobody was forcing Mary Barnes to go riding with him, Tom thought. But still, if it weren't for Prohibition, a man like that wouldn't have had a reason to drive his fancy automobile all the way to Nathan's Mill.

That night Tom slept fitfully, and as soon as faint gray light showed through the loft windows, he got up and dressed in the new shirt and pants Pa had bought him at the clothing bureau. Then he worked on his jaybird carving until he heard Pa stirring downstairs.

Trying not to splash water on his pants legs or dirty his new plaid shirt, Tom did his morning chores. It seemed to take longer than usual for the corn bread to bake, and when it was ready, he was almost too nervous to eat. Finally it was time to leave for school, and he set off, carrying a large wedge of corn bread and an apple in his lunch bucket.

As he approached the footlog at Jenkins Branch, Tom saw Cat Johnson's three little boys hurrying along the wagon road toward the mission. Worried that he was late, Tom walked faster, but when he arrived at the mission, everyone was still outside. His eyes moved from a group of girls who sat demurely on the steps of the schoolhouse-chapel to their little sisters, who were chasing Cat's sons.

Then, to his relief, he saw a couple of boys from Ox Gore Hollow who were about his age. They were playing mumblety-peg at the edge of the clearing while some younger boys watched. Everyone was barefoot, but neatly dressed in outfits from the clothing bureau.

Suddenly all activity stopped and everyone fell quiet as Mrs. Taylor came toward them. She smiled warmly and greeted each child by name, and silently they followed her inside, the little ones clinging to their older brothers and sisters. Tom felt strange, walking alone.

In a few minutes Mrs. Taylor had them arranged in order of size, and Tom found himself sitting on a bench in the back, near two boys from Ox Gore Hollow. The morning passed in a blur. When Mrs. Taylor found out Tom already knew his letters, she put him to work helping the younger children. Later, she gave him some cards, each with a letter and a picture, and showed him how to use them to learn the sounds the letters made.

Tom's head began to swim. This was going to be harder than he'd thought. But he bent over his work, and when Mrs. Taylor came to check on his progress in the afternoon, he was able to tell her the sounds of nearly all the letters. Mrs. Taylor beamed, and Tom quickly looked down. No one had ever smiled on him like that before—not even his own ma. When he raised his eyes again, he saw the boys on the next bench scowling at him.

At the end of the day, Mrs. Taylor praised the students for their hard work and sent them home. But as Tom started out the door, she called him to the front of the room. "I couldn't help but notice the looks the other boys gave you when you did such a good job with the letter sounds," she said.

"They think I'm gittin' a big head," Tom muttered, studying the floor.

"Look at me, Tom," Mrs. Taylor said, waiting until he reluctantly met her eyes. "You mustn't let those boys hold you back from learning as much as you can. And you mustn't let *anybody* hold you back from living the very best life you can. Do you know what I mean?"

Tom shook his head, genuinely puzzled.

"Never mind," Mrs. Taylor said, smiling. "Now don't forget to stop by the mission house and see your dog before you start home each day."

Tom bolted out the door. Not only was he learning to read, he'd be able to see Princess every day after school! As he walked toward the mission house, Princess ran to meet him, then turned and tore back to Amy. "Here, girl," Tom called, and the little dog raced back to him, bounding away again when Amy whistled.

"Play with her on the wagon road," Mrs. Taylor said, pausing on her way back from the schoolhouse-chapel. "Remember, Amy, if you want to keep Tom's dog for him, you can't let her make all this commotion near the house."

Their game was even more fun on the grassy road, and Princess dashed back and forth between them until she dropped to the ground, panting and exhausted. Amy scooped her up. "I haven't had that much fun since I came here," she declared. Her braid had come undone, and her hair hung about her flushed face in long, ripply waves. "Come and have a glass of lemonade before you start home," she said.

Tom stole a sideways glance at Amy as he walked beside her. It was hard to believe she was the same girl who had fussed at him and Lonny after church yesterday.

19

"About time you got yourself down here," Pa growled when Tom joined him at the still Saturday morning. Pa's eyes were red from lack of sleep, and his face was stubbled.

"What you want me to do now I'm here?" Tom asked. He was used to Pa being short-tempered when he was running moonshine.

Pa gestured to the jars of peach brandy lined up by the mash barrels and said, "Take one of them over to the Widow Brown. An' come straight back, you hear?"

"I hear," Tom said, slipping a jar into a sack. As soon as he was out of sight, he began to run. He'd save a little time for a visit with Mrs. Brown, and Pa would never know.

When he came out of the woods onto the path, Tom turned downhill, heading toward the footlog. But before he'd gone far, he heard someone riding toward him. The laurel grew so thickly along both sides of the path that his only escape was to backtrack, and he didn't want to lose the time. Instead, he shoved his sack into a laurel thicket and sat down on the opposite side of the path, cradling his foot in his hands.

"Tom! What's the matter?" Amy cried as she came around a bend and saw him.

He screwed his face into what he hoped was an expression of pain and said "I just stubbed my toe on a big ol' rock."

Amy brought Agamemnon even with him and dismounted. "Get on. You can ride the rest of the way home."

Tom shook his head. "I'll be all right in a minute."

"Then I'll wait and walk along with you."

He should have dashed up the path and slipped into the woods until Amy rode past, Tom thought miserably. Now he'd have to leave Mrs. Brown's brandy and walk all the way—

"Listen," Amy said, "I hear somebody coming."

Tom's heart began to pound when he saw P. D. Hudson approaching on his fine black horse. Stopping in front of them, Hudson looked from Tom to Amy and back to Tom. "This here's Amy, Preacher Taylor's girl," Tom said, trying to keep his voice steady. He turned to Amy and said, "Mr. Hudson's the revenuer your pa sent up to our cabin a while back."

Amy's face reddened, but all she said was, "I'm pleased to meet you, Mr. Hudson."

Hudson's eyes were searching the sides of the trail, and suddenly he made a triumphant sound. Dismounting, he headed for the thicket where Tom had hidden the peach brandy, and reaching into the laurel, he pulled out the sack. "I don't suppose you'd know anything about this, would you?" he asked sarcastically, lifting out the jar.

But Tom had an answer ready. "It's for my pa," he said. "He never promised he wouldn't *drink* moonshine." Tom thanked his lucky stars that Amy didn't know he'd been headed away from home.

Hudson unscrewed the lid and emptied the jar. "Peach brandy," he commented, sniffing.

"When I was riding over in Ox Gore Hollow yesterday,

I saw a really big peach orchard, Mr. Hudson," Amy said eagerly.

The revenuer gave her an appraising look as he hauled himself into the saddle, and then he rode off without a word.

"Well!" Amy said. "He could use a lesson in manners." Then she turned to Tom and said accusingly, "You didn't hurt your foot at all, did you?"

He shook his head. That was twice now Amy had caught him in a lie, and both times it was because of moonshine.

"I hate liars."

"Wal, I don't think much of busybodies."

"Are you calling me a busybody, Tom Higgins?"

Tom shrugged. "What else should I call you, after you set a revenuer on that man over in Ox Gore Holler?"

A look of triumph flashed across Amy's face. "So I was right!" A moment later she was guiding Agamemnon down the trail, calling, "Mr. Hudson? Mr. Hud—son!"

Tom's shoulders drooped. Why hadn't anybody fired the shots to warn that a revenuer was around? And what would Pa do when he found out about this? "One thing sure, he ain't gonna say a word about the clever way I threw Petey Hudson an' Amy off the track," Tom muttered. Picking up the sack and the empty jar, he started slowly back to the still.

That afternoon, he sat slumped on the porch step, still smarting from Pa's tongue-lashing and nursing a smoldering anger at Amy. She'd lie, too, if it meant protecting her pa, he thought. He lifted his head when he heard a high-pitched "Hoo-hoo!" But by the time Amy rode up to the gate he was staring morosely at the ground. He didn't answer when she called to him, and he didn't look up when he heard the gate close behind her.

"I don't blame you for being mad at me, Tom. I came to apologize. You know I don't hate you—I like you a lot."

Tom blushed scarlet. "I still think you're a busybody," he said without looking up. "An' so's your pa."

The step creaked as Amy sat down beside him. "You're still mad at me," she said flatly.

Tom nodded. He knew it wasn't her fault Pa had been so hard on him, but he wasn't quite ready to forgive her for calling him a liar. He scowled, remembering how ugly the word had sounded when she spit it out at him.

The step creaked again as Amy stood up. "Well, I'll see you at church tomorrow," she said. "I hope you won't still be mad."

He'd still be mad, Tom decided as he watched her leave. Or at least he'd let her think he was.

20

The fragrance of apples hung heavy in the air as Tom cranked the cider mill. The only good thing that had happened all week was discovering that a couple of trees in the overgrown orchard at the old homesite had produced a bumper crop of summer apples, he thought.

Tom swatted at one of the hornets that buzzed around the fruit he was grinding. He'd hoped that the papery gray nest hanging from a branch at the far edge of the clearing was an old, abandoned one, but obviously it wasn't. He poured more apples into the hopper of the cider mill and was about to start grinding again when he heard something crashing toward him through the woods. His hand froze on the crank, but his mind raced. What could it be?

Peering through the screening branches of the uprooted pine, Tom saw Princess burst into the clearing, her nose to the ground and her tail wagging. She must have tracked him from the wagon road—he'd taken a sack of apples to the Widow Brown before he'd started work this morning. When Tom gave a low whistle, the little dog's head came up and she bounded across the clearing and around the fallen tree. She leaped up into his outstretched arms, and he hugged her while she licked his face.

Suddenly, though, Princess cocked her head, and a moment later Tom heard a faint voice. It was Amy, calling Princess, and the little dog yapped in response. Wiggling out of his arms, she ran toward the sound of Amy's voice.

"Good thing she left," Tom muttered as he watched Princess disappear into the woods, "or Amy might of come lookin' for her." He began to crank the cider mill again, but to his dismay, a few minutes later he heard Princess coming back. She was going to lead Amy straight to him—straight to Pa's still! What would Pa say when he found out?

This time, when Princess ran to him, Tom held her muzzle so she couldn't bark. She squirmed and clawed at his hands, making smothered little sounds while he hoped that Amy wouldn't find her way through the thicket. But now her voice sounded closer, and Tom knew that she had found the maze of paths he and Pa had chopped as escape routes if they had to flee the revenuers.

He had to stop Amy! Suddenly, Tom thought of a way

to make her turn back. Letting Princess go, he reached into his back pocket for his slingshot and the rounded stones he'd picked up on his way down the path. Fitting a stone into the sling, he drew back the band and aimed at the hornets' nest. He missed, swore silently, and aimed again just as Princess burst back into the clearing for the third time.

"Princess! Come back!" Amy's voice was so close that Tom knew this shot had to count. Holding his breath, he let the stone fly. It was a solid hit, and angry insects poured from the bobbing gray sphere just as Princess bounded around the edge of the uprooted tree. Tom grabbed her and peered between the branches, poised for flight. If the hornets didn't scare Amy away, he'd have to run into the woods behind him. He'd cut to one side and then let Princess go, hoping—

"Princess? Where are you?" Amy sounded close to tears. As she came into the clearing, she stopped to swat at one of the hornets and then began to back up, waving her hands in front of her face.

It was working! Tom could hardly believe his good luck—she was going back! But when Amy cried out, he felt terrible. He'd only meant to turn her back, not to hurt her. She cried out again, then turned and ran. Princess struggled free and tore after her. As the little dog raced across the clearing and into the woods, Tom waited for the yap of pain that would tell him she'd been stung, too. But all he heard was more cries from Amy, each one a little fainter, until at last all was quiet.

Woodenly, Tom set to work again. He welcomed the monotonous grumble of the cider mill and the calming effect of his rhythmic cranking. But his earlier excitement about making apple brandy was gone now, replaced by worry.

What if Princess came back to look for him when Pa was here? What if *Amy* found her way back again? Would she figure out that Princess had been tracking him? Did she already suspect that the maze of trails she'd followed through the laurel had been made by a moonshiner? Suddenly Tom stopped cranking. He'd have to tell Pa.

There was a leaden feeling in Tom's stomach, a certainty that Pa would never trust him again. And why should he? After all, this was the second time the still had been discovered because of him. Tom sighed. He should have put the apples through the cider mill before he went to Mrs. Brown's cabin. Then Princess wouldn't have been able to track him. Or, Tom reasoned, she might have led Amy to the still after he'd gone. He wouldn't have known anything about that, so he couldn't have told Pa.

Tom began to crank the cider mill with renewed energy. He'd pretend that was what had happened. Pa would see the paw prints and footprints tomorrow and know the still had been discovered. He'd be angry, all right, but not as angry as he'd be if he knew the whole story. Tom felt a little uneasy about deceiving Pa, but he reminded himself that Pa never gave a second thought to tricking somebody when it suited him. It was just that Pa did it with words, and he was doing it with silence.

Tom wiped the sweat from his forehead and began to pour more apples into the mill. A sudden fiery pain on his wrist made him drop the basket, and as apples rained down and rolled away, he brushed off a hornet and ran to plunge his arm into the spring. Even though the water was icy cold, Tom's wrist still felt as if it were burning.

"I deserved this," he muttered, feeling even worse about what he'd done to Amy.

It wasn't until the preacher fumbled in his pocket for the pitch pipe the next morning that Tom realized Mrs. Taylor wasn't at church. Glancing toward the end of the front row, he saw that Amy was missing, too. He looked down at his swollen wrist and felt a stir of apprehension. Then, to his dismay, Preacher Taylor began the service by asking the congregation to remember Amy in their prayers.

"Her face and arms were badly stung by some kind of bees yesterday when she was in the woods looking for her little dog," he said, "and the doctor in Buckton has gone to Roanoke for a funeral."

The preacher had ridden to town for the doctor! No one went for the doctor unless they were afraid a person would die. Was Amy going to die? Tom hardly heard a word of the sermon. He was too busy worrying—and wishing he hadn't avoided Amy all week, letting her think he was still mad.

Tom stood as the congregation struggled through the last hymn with the people in the back rows several beats behind those in the front. The preacher sang loudly, but that was no substitute for Mrs. Taylor's keeping time as she led the singing.

Outside after the service, Tom waited near the edge of the clearing, sure that today the preacher would go straight home instead of staying to talk. Tom fell into step beside him as he walked purposefully past the little clusters of people and headed toward the mission house. "Preacher

Taylor," he said, "I been thinkin' maybe Miz Brown can do something for Amy."

"What could she possibly do that Amy's mother isn't already doing?" the preacher asked impatiently.

"She's got potions for 'most everything," Tom said, practically running to keep up. "Folks 'round here always call on her when they're feelin' poorly."

Preacher Taylor walked still faster. "I'm sure you mean well, Tom, but I won't allow anyone to practice ignorant backwoods superstitions on my daughter."

Tom felt as though he'd been smacked in the face. Without another word, he turned around, and kicking at a twig, he muttered, "Them ignorant backwoods superstitions have done more for folks 'round here than all that preacher's talkin' has. Or ever will."

Back at the schoolhouse-chapel, Andy called to Tom. "Mrs. Brown invited you and your pa for dinner," he said. "They were in a hurry to leave, so I waited to tell you."

As they started down the wagon road together Tom said, "I ain't never heard of sendin' for the doctor for nothin' but bee stings."

"If you're stung often enough, it can be almost as serious as being bitten by a poisonous snake," Andy replied.

As serious as being snake bit! What had he done? "You think Amy's gonna die?" Tom asked fearfully.

"No, but I imagine she's feeling pretty miserable."

They walked the rest of the way in silence. When they arrived at Mrs. Brown's cabin, the old woman was busily preparing the meal, but Pa was nowhere to be seen. He was checking the still, Tom realized. Suddenly, his mouth felt dry, and he wished he'd told Pa about what had happened the day before.

Andy played his banjo and sang while Mrs. Brown cooked, but Tom couldn't listen. When Pa finally joined them, he sat silently on the porch, and Tom was pretty sure he wasn't listening, either.

At last Mrs. Brown called them in to dinner. Tom breathed in the aroma of fried ham slices and boiled vegetables and wondered how he could be so hungry at a time like this. He let his eyes wander over the cloth-covered table, taking in the dishes of corn relish and cucumber pickles and clabber cheese and apple butter. We'd eat like this, too, he thought, if only Ma hadn't left.

"Wal," Pa announced grimly, "I'm gonna have to move my still again. Them bees that stung the preacher's li'l gal was hornets from a big ol' nest near my rig. There's paw prints all 'round the still from that mutt of hers, an' footprints right up to the edge of the clearin'. I moved out the still pot an' the worm an' hid 'em."

Tom watched the butter melt into a golden puddle on his mashed potatoes and wondered just how much Pa suspected.

"This is the second time that li'l gal's stumbled on my still, with a bit of help from her critters," Pa said. "Looked like that mutt of hers tracked Tom from the wagon road." He glared across the table at Tom and asked, "What was you doin' there when you was supposed to be grindin' that fruit?"

"He brought me some summer apples so's I could make you a pie, June," Mrs. Brown said. "We'll have it for dessert."

Silently, Tom thanked the old woman for coming to his rescue. They both knew Pa's weakness for apple pie.

"You know, June, you can set up your rig on my property if you want to. Nobody'd have a second thought if they saw you or the boy comin' here, and I could give a shout if a revenuer was 'round," Mrs. Brown added.

Pa looked relieved. "We'll look for a place after dinner, then," he said. "Andy, you can come with us, if you want."

"I'd like to work with you while you set up the new still and do a run of brandy," Andy said. "That way I could have a chapter in my book on making moonshine the old-fashioned way."

Pa's quick agreement told Tom how much his father trusted Andy. It was hard to believe that not long ago he'd been a stranger they thought might be a revenuer.

They had just finished the apple pie when they heard a holler. "That sounds like Miz Taylor," Mrs. Brown said in surprise. Tom was halfway to the gate and the old woman was on the porch by the time the preacher's wife rode up on Agamemnon.

"I came to see if you can do anything for Amy," she called to Mrs. Brown, her words coming in a rush.

"I'll git my potions," the old woman said, hurrying back inside.

Mrs. Taylor looked down at Tom. "I want to thank you for suggesting to my husband that Mrs. Brown might be able to help Amy."

"But I thought he didn't cotton to ignorant backwoods superstitions," Tom said, puzzled.

Mrs. Taylor's eyes flashed. "Herb women were easing people's suffering long before anyone even heard of doctors. Or preachers, either," she said shortly.

Andy followed Mrs. Brown to the gate and lifted her onto Agamemnon, and Mrs. Taylor wrapped her arm protectively around the old woman and turned the horse toward the mission.

"Wal," Pa said as the dust settled behind them, "while she's gone, we might as well look for a place for that still."

Tom followed the men through the woods, but his heart wasn't in it. His steps began to lag, and soon he fell behind, but no one seemed to notice. If Pa didn't care whether he was there or not, he might as well go back, Tom decided. After what had happened yesterday, he could use a little time away from everything that had to do with stilling.

Tom waited on the Widow Brown's porch for a while, hoping to find out if the old woman had been able to help Amy. Then he took a stick and scratched a message in the dirt outside her gate: I HAF GON HOM. But when he reached the wagon road he paused for a moment and then turned toward the mission. As he drew near the house, he saw someone on the porch. It was the preacher, sitting with his head bowed.

At school the next morning, Tom's eyes searched Mrs. Taylor's face, and she gave him a reassuring smile. Even so, he had trouble keeping his mind on his work, and at noon he had to stay in his seat to finish the last arithmetic problem before he took his lunch bucket and joined the others. Mrs. Taylor stopped beside him on her way out.

"Mrs. Brown's potion made Amy feel ever so much better," she said. "I thought you'd want to know."

Pulling his chipmunk carving from his pocket, Tom asked, "Can you take her this? An' tell her"—he hesitated, blushing furiously—"tell her I said she ain't no busybody."

"I'll tell her that," Mrs. Taylor said, stroking the carved animal with her finger. "Who made this lovely thing, Tom?"

"I did, ma'am," he said.

"You amaze me! You're as talented as you are smart."

Blushing again, Tom stared at his slate and waited for her to leave. Then, his shoulders back and his head held high, he took his lunch bucket and went outside to join the other boys.

21

Tom was surprised to see Andy coming toward the Widow Brown's gate in response to his holler.

"Mrs. Brown's gone off to Ox Gore Hollow to bring another little Cobbin into the world," Andy said. "Is there anything I can do for you?"

Tom's shoulders drooped. "Can I wait for her?"

"Sure, but it might be a while." Andy led the way back to the porch and picked up his banjo.

Tom slumped down into Mrs. Brown's rocking chair, reminded of how he'd sat there on Sunday, worrying about Amy and about whether Pa would figure out what had really happened at the still. And here he was again, still worrying.

Andy stopped playing and laid the banjo across his lap. "Something's bothering you," he said.

Tom nodded, wondering how Andy and Mrs. Taylor could see that, but Pa hadn't noticed. Without raising his eyes, Tom whispered, "I done somethin' awful, Andy."

"Is it something you can make amends for? Something you can make right again?"

"Ain't no way I can make it right," Tom said, wishing he could. And then, in a rush of words, he told Andy how he had been responsible for Amy's stings. "I know she's gittin' better, but every time I think about it, an' every time I see Miz Taylor, I feel bad all over again," he finished. "You think I should own up to what I done?"

Andy frowned and asked, "Own up to Amy, or own up to your pa?"

Tom just looked at him. He'd meant own up to Mrs. Taylor.

"Do you think it would make Amy feel better if she knew the truth?" Andy asked.

"It would make her feel worse!"

After a moment Andy said, "I think if Amy knew you'd been involved in what happened, then you'd want to explain and ask her forgiveness. But since she doesn't know, you'll have to forgive yourself instead of burdening her with your regret."

Or burdening Mrs. Taylor, Tom thought. "But how do you forgive yourself?"

"It takes time," Andy said, "but the first step is to stop going over and over the whole thing in your mind."

"How'd you know I was doin' that?" Tom asked in surprise.

"Because I know human nature. And the human condition."

"The human condition? What's that?"

Andy seemed to be concentrating on lighting his pipe, but finally he said, "It's what all people have in common, no matter where they live. Or when they live. It's what makes the story of the Greek kings leading their armies against the Trojans as gripping today as when it was first told, almost three thousand years ago. And it's what will make people all over this vast country respond to the stories and ballads from these hills. Do you understand what I'm saying, Tom?"

Tom didn't understand at all, but he wasn't going to disappoint Andy by admitting it. "I'm gonna have to think on it awhile," he said. "You ain't gonna let on to Pa about what I done, are you?"

"The only way your pa will find out is if you tell him yourself."

"Then he ain't gonna find out."

Andy puffed on his pipe and studied Tom for a long time before he asked, "Are you afraid of what he might do to you if he knew?"

Staring down at his feet, Tom said, "I'm worried about what he might think of me. This is twice now somethin' I done led Amy right to the still. No moonshiner wants a son who can't do no better 'n that."

"It sounds to me like you tried your best to do the right thing this time."

Tom looked up and said, "Seems like no matter how hard I try, I can't please Pa."

"One thing I've learned in the short time I've been working with your pa is that making moonshine's a difficult and dangerous business," Andy said. "When a single careless move can mean a year in jail, there's not much room for making mistakes."

Tom had never looked at it that way. "I guess you're right, Andy," he said slowly. "But how come he don't ever notice when I do somethin' right?"

After a pause Andy said, "Some fathers find it hard to show approval. Discipline is the only way they know to show they care."

"Then Pa must care a heck of a lot about me," Tom joked.

But Andy took him seriously. "I'm sure he does. And with good reason—you're a boy any father would be proud of."

Blushing furiously, Tom muttered, "I gotta git on home. I'll see Miz Brown some other time."

Andy's words echoed in Tom's mind as he hurried down the path toward the wagon road, but beneath the surprised pleasure they gave him was a deep sadness. Why couldn't *Pa* have said that? Probably because he didn't feel that way, Tom decided. Andy thought Pa cared, but how would Andy know?

" 'Cause he's always watchin'," Tom said aloud. After all, Andy had seen that something was bothering him, and he'd said he knew human nature. *Could Andy be right?*

Thoughtfully, Tom stepped onto the footlog. Talking to Andy had settled one thing, anyway. He was going to stop thinking about what had happened at the still, and he wasn't ever going to tell anyone about it. At least not till he was grown and had a son of his own and was passing on to him the art of making moonshine.

22

On Friday, Amy was waiting by the fence when school let out. "Tom!" she called. "Can I talk to you for a minute?"

Tom went to meet her, glad to see for himself that she had recovered from her stings. He'd stopped blaming himself, but he couldn't help wondering if Amy would still want to talk to him if she knew he'd been responsible for her suffering. He bent down to pet Princess, who had tangled herself up in the rope Amy was using as a leash.

"How come you've got her on a rope?" Tom asked, trying to keep the little dog from winding it around his ankles.

Looking embarrassed, Amy said, "Father won't let me take her for a walk without it. You see, I followed her when she ran into the woods, even though I'd promised not to go off the trails." Amy lowered her voice and added, "Father was furious. He said getting stung was my punishment for disobedience, but Mother says that's hogwash."

Tom thought of the preacher sitting alone on the porch of the mission house, his head in his hands, while the Widow Brown was inside with Amy. He hadn't looked furious then. Did some fathers find it hard to show they were worried?

"I think it's hogwash, too," Tom said, realizing that Amy was waiting for him to say something. "What did you want to talk to me about?" He was ready to change the subject before it got any more personal.

"I wanted to thank you for the chipmunk carving you gave me," Amy said. "I just love it. And now I have something for you, too." She held out a book with a picture of a fox and a crow on the cover. "I think you'll like this. It's called *Aesop's Fables,* and it's full of stories."

Tom held the book almost reverently. "Can I keep it till I've read 'em all?" he asked.

"You can keep it always," Amy said. "I want you to have it to remember me by."

Tom frowned and repeated, "To remember you by?"

"I'm leaving for boarding school tomorrow," she explained.

"Boardin' school? T'morrer?" he echoed numbly.

Amy nodded. "I'll be a scholarship student at a church school. That means my parents won't have to pay to send me there. I would have told you sooner, Tom, but first you were still mad at me, and then I didn't want you to see how awful I looked swollen up with those ugly stings. Don't look so sad, Tom. I'll be back for Christmas."

Tom forced a weak smile and said, "It'll probably take me till Christmas to finish all them stories, seein' as I read right slow." He looked away, thinking that he should have known a girl like Amy wouldn't stay here, that she'd be going back to where she belonged.

"Do you want to go to that boardin' school, Amy?" he asked.

"I looked forward to it all summer, but now I'm feeling a little scared," she confessed. "I've never been away from home before." Then, as though trying to convince herself, she added, "Father says it will be a good experience for me, and that I shouldn't underestimate the importance of education in planning my future."

Tom could almost hear Preacher Taylor saying those very words, but what exactly did he mean about planning her future?

"What about you, Tom? What will you be when you grow up?"

"I'll be a man, of course."

139

"I know that," Amy said impatiently. "I mean what kind of work will you do?"

" 'Round here, you mostly do what your pa does," Tom said. "The Nathan boys will work at the mill with their pa, an' when they're not farmin', Lonny Rigsby an' his brothers will be carpenters. Harry Perkins will be a cooper—he's already helpin' his pa make barrels. Each man passes on his craft to his sons."

"So what about you?"

Tom heard the note of challenge in Amy's voice. "I'm a moonshiner's son," he said quietly, meeting her eyes.

A flush of pink spread across Amy's face. "How can you stand here and tell me you're going to be a moonshiner when you know how I feel about the evils of drink?" Her hands were clenched in tight little fists.

"You git mad when I lie to you," Tom said reasonably.

"But why can't you do some kind of honest work?"

"There ain't nothin' dishonest about moonshinin'," Tom objected. "Not unless you're contaminatin' your likker or sellin' three-day-old likker for aged whiskey. If you take pride in your product and treat your customers fair, makin' moonshine's as honest a craft as any other."

Amy faced him, her eyes flashing. "You're impossible, just impossible! And besides, if you're a moonshiner's son, that must mean your father's still making liquor after he promised the judge he wouldn't. You have your nerve, talking to me about honesty, Tom Higgins!"

Princess danced between them, barking nervously and looking from Amy to Tom, but for once they both ignored her.

"Anybody 'round here can tell you, my pa don't go back on his word," Tom said. "He promised that judge he wouldn't make corn likker, and he ain't made corn likker. And he ain't *gonna* make corn likker ever again as long as he lives. An' that's a fact. My pa's a honest man, an' I don't want to hear you sayin' he ain't."

Amy had backed away from him, and Tom realized he'd been shaking his finger at her.

"I guess I got carried away again, Tom. I'm sorry," she said quietly, reaching down to calm Princess.

That was one of the things Tom liked best about Amy— she never stayed mad long, and when she was wrong, she said so. But this time, she wasn't all that wrong. Pa wasn't exactly breaking his word, but if that judge had known Junior Higgins was simply going to switch from corn liquor to fruit brandy, Pa would be in jail now. Confused, Tom walked away, clutching his book and half fearing, half wishing that Amy would call to him.

By the time he reached the footlog, Tom was miserable. He didn't feel at all clever about the way he'd made Amy believe Pa had given up making moonshine when he'd only given up making corn whiskey. And he wished he hadn't walked off like that without so much as a good-bye. After all, it would be three long months before he saw Amy again.

23

Tom and Pa were the last to arrive at the Johnsons' house for the work party. Most of the neighbors were already sitting in the shade near several tubs of green beans. Andy was already writing in his notebook, Tom noticed as he made his way toward Lonny and Harry.

Soon everyone was busily snapping the ends off the beans and breaking them in half while Jonah Simpson told a tale. Just as he finished, Preacher Taylor rode past on Odysseus, slowing the horse to a walk at the sight of the crowd gathered in the yard.

"C'mon in, Preacher," Cat Johnson called as he tipped a bushel basket over the jar of peach brandy that was being passed around. "We can use your help here."

Tom watched Preacher Taylor tie his horse and come into the yard, and he wondered what Cat was up to. The preacher hesitated when he saw everyone at work and said, "I, ah, I thought you meant spiritual help," but he allowed himself to be drawn into the group. "What's going on?" he asked, sitting down next to Tom.

"This here's a bean stringin'," Tom said. "Take this here needle, run it through them beans, an' pull 'em onto the thread," he instructed, pointing to a panful of beans that had been snapped in half. "Not longwise, Preacher. Crosswise."

Raising her voice so she could be heard above the smothered laughter, Lonny's mother said, "We hang up long strings of them beans to dry, an' come winter, we cut some of 'em down and cook 'em half a day in a big pot of water with a hunk of salt pork. Mmm, mmm!"

Tom grinned at the preacher's awkwardness, but his attention quickly shifted to the Widow Brown as she began to tell her story. Even the smallest children sat in rapt attention as the old woman told how clever Jack had outwitted the king and won the girl he loved for a wife.

When she had finished, Cat Johnson, a wicked glint in

his eye, turned to the preacher. "Preacher Taylor, we'd like to hear one of your stories now."

Looking pleased that he'd been asked—and relieved to have an excuse to put aside the beans—the preacher said, "My story's about Joseph and the coat of many colors, and—"

"That ain't *your* story," Cat objected, "that's a Bible story. Tell us one of your own."

Looking uncomfortable, Preacher Taylor said, "But I don't have any stories of my own. I'm not a storyteller like Mrs. Brown."

Tom was wishing Pa would rescue the preacher by offering to tell his tale when beside him Harry called out, "I bet you Tom's got a story, Mr. Johnson. Why don't you ask him to tell us one?"

All eyes turned expectantly toward Tom, and he was filled with self-conscious confusion. Harry would pay for this!

"How about it, Tom? Makes sense that June's boy might have a story or two up his sleeve," Cat Johnson said.

Tom's face burned. It was bad enough to be embarrassed on his own account, without having Pa brought into it. But then, in a rush of excitement, he remembered the book Amy had given him. He'd show them! He wouldn't sit there tongue-tied and be humiliated in front of everyone—in front of Pa.

Scrambling to his feet, Tom held his right arm out from his body and gave it a shake.

"Whatcha doin' that for, Tom?" asked one of Cat's little boys.

"Why, I'm tryin' to git a story down out of my sleeve," he said, shaking his arm again. "Ah, here's one." Sitting down, Tom said, "This here story tells about somethin' that happened in Buckton a while ago. Lots of folks there raised sheep back then, an' they hired Wiley, the sheriff's son, to drive 'em to a pasture just outside town each mornin'. Wiley, he was supposed to stay all day an' watch over them sheep, 'cause there was wolves that lived not far from town."

Tom was pleased that his voice showed none of his nervousness. "Now, at first Wiley felt proud of havin' a job of work like that, but after a while it got right tiresome, so he decided to have him a little fun. He left them sheep all grazin' an' headed on back to Buckton. Soon as he got in sight of town, he commenced runnin' and hollerin', 'Wolf! Wolf!'

"When folks heard him, they all grabbed whatever they had handy an' started for the pasture. The women ran out of their houses carryin' skillets, the storekeeper brought a shovel, the judge had that wooden hammer of his, an' behind 'em all came their preacher, armed with his prayers. The sheriff an' his deputies weren't 'round to help that day, you see, 'cause they was all over in Bad Camp Holler, lookin' for moonshine stills."

After the howls of laughter died down, Tom went on. " 'Course, when they all got to the pasture, them sheep was grazin' peaceful like, an' there weren't no wolf in sight. Them folks couldn't understand it at all—till they saw ol' Wiley, laughin' his head off. Now, the storekeeper an' the judge an' the preacher, they walked on back to Buckton, grumblin' all the way about how that boy's pa should tan his hide, but them women chased Wiley all the way home."

"Good for them," Lonny's ma said.

Tom couldn't believe how well he was doing! "Wiley, he found out there was worse things than tiresome—like gittin' whacked with skillets—so next day he took his knife with him when he drove them sheep out to the pasture. He was whittlin' away on a stick when a whole pack of wolves came in sight. Wiley, he ran back to town, lickety-split, hollerin', 'Wolf! Wolf!'

"The sheriff an' his deputies came runnin' down Main Street with their guns, but everybody said, 'Don't you pay no attention to Wiley, he pulled this trick yesterday.' An' no matter how hard Wiley begged, nobody would go back to the pasture. That pack of wolves killed every one of them sheep—an' that weren't the worst of it. Everybody started blamin' everybody else for what happened, an' things was in a right sorry state till they all agreed never to mention it again as long as they lived."

Tom looked at his listeners and said simply, "I guess that's why none of you folks knew about all this till I told you just now." He was almost startled by the cheers and clapping. Harry put two fingers in his mouth and gave a shrill whistle, and Lonny pounded on the half-empty tub of beans.

Tom was elated. He'd done it! He'd told a tale, just like Pa. He flashed a proud look in his father's direction, but Pa was bent over the beans he was snapping.

Cat Johnson raised his voice above the clamor and said, "Folks, we have a new storyteller in these parts, an' we have Harry Perkins to thank for bringin' him to our attention."

Tom made a face at Harry and decided he wouldn't bother trying to get even with him after all, because in a way, he already had. And then the preacher was shaking his hand and congratulating him. "You've done something I couldn't do, Tom," the preacher said ruefully, standing up. Tom watched him mount Odysseus and ride away. Cat Johnson shouldn't have made sport of Preacher Taylor, he thought.

Later, after everyone had eaten their fill of the meal the women served, Cat announced, "Wal, folks, we've saved the best for last. June Higgins, here, is gonna tell us his tale now."

There was a murmur of anticipation, and Harry leaned toward Tom and said, "Don't look like he's got much cause to worry about competition from the likes of you."

Tom jabbed Harry with his elbow, but as he began to lose himself in the magic of Pa's storytelling, he knew that though his friend's words were meant as a jibe, they were the honest truth.

When Pa's story ended, there was hushed silence. Finally, Cat Johnson cleared his throat and said, "Wal, folks, I was right about savin' the best for last, wasn't I?"

The spell was broken, and Ol' Man Barnes declared, "Ain't nobody can tell a tale like June Higgins." After chorusing their agreement, people began to say their good-byes and light their lanterns for the walk home. Tom waited until he saw Pa glance around, looking for him, before he left the shadows.

"Here's our newest storyteller!" Cat exclaimed, clapping him on the shoulder. "Got any more tales up your sleeve?"

"I'll have to look in my other shirt," Tom said, grinning.

As they started home Pa asked, "Where'd you git that wolf story?"

"From the book Amy gave me. 'Course, I changed it

some." Tom waited expectantly, but Pa's only response was a grunt.

Tom struggled against the disappointment that threatened to blind him with tears. Everyone else had liked his story. Lonny and Harry had obviously been impressed, Mrs. Brown had said she was proud of him, and Andy — But none of that mattered if Pa wasn't pleased.

Suddenly Pa broke the silence. "Tellin' a tale is a art. Next time, don't make a fool of yourself with that business about your sleeve."

So that was it. A feeling of relief swept through Tom. Pa's criticism stung, but at least it hadn't been his storytelling that had made him look foolish in Pa's eyes. Someday, somehow, Tom promised himself, he'd make Pa proud of him.

24

"Now you make sure you say exactly what I told you when you take Ol' Man Barnes that message after school, you hear?" Pa called.

"I hear!" Tom hurled the words over his shoulder as he went out the gate. He'd repeated it perfectly three times, hadn't he? But just the same, he rehearsed it on his way down to the mission and again whenever he thought about it during the day.

To Tom's surprise, the store was deserted when he arrived at the settlement after school. "An' what can I do for you today, young feller?" Ol' Man Barnes asked, looking up from the newspaper he was reading.

"I have a message from Pa," Tom said, closing his eyes and reciting, "Tell Mary to let her boyfriend know that Eddie Jarvis might be double-crossin' him an' sellin' his moonshine to another bootlegger. An' after she's done that, tell Eddie Jarvis that King Higgins has set Big Jim on him."

Ol' Man Barnes listened intently, and after he'd repeated it back to Tom he said, "Your pa works fast. It was just yesterday Eddie came in here drunk as a bat, braggin' on how he'd met that revenuer a couple months back an' told him June Higgins had a still in his woods. 'Course, Lance Rigsby was on his way up to your place 'most before the words was out of Eddie's mouth."

"No need for Pa to wait once he had that kind of proof Eddie done it," Tom said, trying to look like he'd known all about this.

"You tell your pa I'll take care of it," the storekeeper called after Tom as he left.

He was nothing but an errand boy, Tom thought as he headed toward the Rigsbys' place. For a while, he'd been sure Pa was starting to look on him more as a partner, especially after he'd built the furnace when they set up the rig at the old homesite. But now that Andy was working at the still while he wrote his chapter on making moonshine, Pa had all the help he needed. Tom sighed. At first he'd been glad to have some free time, but now he was beginning to feel left out.

Tom turned into the Rigsbys' lane, reminding himself that if he were working with Pa, he wouldn't be able to visit his friend. He waved when he saw Lonny and his father each planing a board clamped to a pair of sawhorses they'd set up in the shade.

"Come on over here, Tom—I want you to look at somethin'," Lance Rigsby called. "Now, what do you think of that?" he asked when Tom joined them.

"Of what?" Tom asked, puzzled.

"Of that planin' job Lonny done. Bet you can't tell the difference between Lonny's board an' mine."

Tom walked around the sawhorses, squinting at the boards they'd been smoothing and running his hand along each of them. Then he stood back and pointed at the one nearest Lonny. "It's easy to tell this is the one done by a beginner," he announced.

Lance frowned, and Lonny looked so crestfallen that Tom had trouble keeping a straight face. Both of them looked at the boards, and Lance ran his hand along first one and then the other. "You don't know what you're talkin' about," he said shortly. "Lonny's done a fine job here!"

"I didn't say he hadn't, Mr. Rigsby," Tom said innocently, "but compared to you, Lonny's a beginner, an' I knew for sure that he done the one he's standin' next to."

Lance Rigsby slapped Tom on the back and said, "You're a chip off the ol' block, you know that? You got the same way with words your pa has."

A warm feeling stole over Tom, and he hoped he wasn't blushing. "What are you gonna make?" he asked Lonny.

"Blanket chest. If it turns out good enough, we'll give it for a present at the next weddin'. If it don't, Ma's got herself a extry one."

"I'd guess it's gonna be good enough for a gift," Tom

said, hoping to make up to Lonny for the joke he'd pulled on him.

Ignoring the compliment, Lonny challenged, "So when do I git to see you workin' with your pa?"

"Tell you what," Tom said, an idea forming in his mind, "you an' Harry meet me after school t'morrer, an' I'll show you where we used to have our rig. You can see what's left of the furnace I made." Pa hadn't seen any reason to destroy the evidence of a still at the old homesite, since there was no way it could be traced to him.

Lonny quickly agreed to the plan, and Tom started home. Some folks didn't know how lucky they were, he thought, remembering the pride in Lance Rigsby's voice when he showed off Lonny's work. "An' all he done was take a tool an' scrape a dumb ol' board till it was smooth," he muttered.

The next afternoon, Tom scuffed through the fallen leaves with Lonny and Harry, wishing he'd never said he'd show them the old still site. Harry's sharp eyes were sure to spot the hornets' nest, and it wouldn't take him long to figure out that—

"Listen," Harry said, breaking the silence.

"Must be the preacher," Lonny said as the pounding hoofbeats grew louder.

Tom shook his head, remembering the message he'd given Ol' Man Barnes the day before. "Preacher Taylor wouldn't ride Odysseus that hard. It's Eddie Jarvis."

"Yeah, Eddie ridin' that bay mare he bought last month," agreed Lonny.

The boys hardly had time to move to the edge of the road before Eddie Jarvis galloped past with a vicious-looking brown dog running alongside him. Tom's stomach contracted when he saw the malevolent look Eddie sent in his direction, and he knew the storekeeper had delivered Pa's message.

"They sure was flyin'," Lonny said as they set off again. "That mean ol' dog couldn't hardly keep up!"

"C'mon," Harry said urgently. "We won't never have another chance like this."

Tom and Lonny looked at each other and then at Harry. "Chance to do what?" Tom asked suspiciously.

"To have a look at Eddie's place."

Grinning, Lonny said, "Yeah! Let's go."

Glad the boys had forgotten about going to the abandoned still site, Tom said, "I'll walk up there with you, but all I'm gonna do is look. I ain't gonna stay an' mess 'round Eddie's place."

"You scared or somethin'?" Harry asked.

"You'd be scared, too, if you had good sense," Tom retorted, feeling prickles of excitement mixed with fear.

"Even if I ain't been to school like some people, I got sense enough to know Eddie can't do me no harm when he ain't there," Harry said scornfully.

"It won't hurt none to poke 'round a little," Lonny said.

Almost without realizing it, the boys had lowered their voices as they turned onto the weed-choked track that led uphill from the wagon road to Eddie's cabin. Even though they knew Eddie wasn't home, their footsteps slowed as they drew near his clearing, and when they saw the cabin, they stopped and stared.

"Ain't much better 'n a pig sty," Harry declared.

Before anyone could answer, the front door swung open and a stranger came out of the ramshackle cabin. The man hesitated when he saw the boys and then walked toward them. Even before Tom recognized him, he knew it had to be the bootlegger.

"I'm a friend of Eddie's," the man said. "Do you know where I can find him?" When Tom shook his head, the bootlegger said, "Well, if you see him, you tell him Big Jim was here looking for him—and tell him I'll be back." He smiled, showing a gold tooth, but his eyes were cold.

The boys were silent until Big Jim was out of sight, and then Harry said, "He's a liar, 'cause Eddie ain't got no friends." His voice rose with excitement as he added, "He's probably a thief come lookin' for the money Eddie gets from that bootlegger."

"Big Jim *is* the bootlegger," Lonny said. "But all them moonshiners load their likker in his car back at the settlement, so what's he doin' over here?"

Tell Eddie that King Higgins set Big Jim on him. There was a hollow feeling in Tom's stomach as the words echoed through his mind. "He's after Eddie," he said.

"Then somebody must of warned him, an' that's why he lit out of here so fast," Lonny said thoughtfully.

Tom looked away, fearful that his face would show too much, and his eye fell on the chain fastened to the corner of the cabin. He felt a new stir of excitement. That chain was long enough for Eddie's dog to guard both the front door and the door of the lean-to kitchen out back. Tom's heart began to beat faster. "I'm gonna have a look in that window," he said, forgetting his earlier fears. "Ain't you comin'?"

Furtively glacing over their shoulders, the boys followed him. Tom gave a start when the sagging porch floor creaked, and then his heart began to pound with excitement. Eddie had hung cornmeal sacks over his windows, and there was only one reason he'd have done that!

Tom's hand trembled as he pressed the latch and pushed the door open. Just as he'd thought! Eddie had his rig set up inside his cabin. He must have moved it there when the revenuers searching through the woods got too close for comfort.

Behind him, Tom heard Lonny say, "Look at the size of that there still pot!"

"Go on in," Harry said. "I dare you."

Tom pulled the door shut. "I'm gonna go 'round to the kitchen door."

Lonny and Harry followed him around the house, but the door to the lean-to kitchen was barred from the inside. "Boost me up to that there window," Tom said, and he stepped into their cupped hands and was lifted high enough to grasp the sill. The window was open, and he pushed aside the filthy sack that served as a curtain. His eyes widened and he stared until, suddenly afraid, he whispered urgently, "Lemme down!" Once on the ground he ran, his friends at his heels, cutting through the woods instead of following the weedy track, and not stopping even when he reached the wagon road.

"What was in there?" Lonny asked, panting, when Tom finally slowed to a walk.

"Sacks of sugar an' cornmeal stacked 'most to the ceilin'," he said, trying to catch his breath.

Harry gave him a puzzled look. "So how come you ran?"

" 'Cause I remembered what could happen to somebody that snoops 'round a man's still," Tom said. He remembered the threatening look Eddie had sent in his direction, too. "You can go back there if you want, but I'm goin' home." Without waiting to see what the other boys would do, Tom started toward the settlement.

"Ain't you goin' the wrong way?" Lonny called, hurrying after him.

"I'm goin' the *long* way. I ain't gonna risk meetin' up with Eddie between here an' the footlog if he decides to come back home." This was one time being June Higgins's son would be a disadvantage.

"You was gonna show us where your pa had his still, don't forget," Harry reminded him.

"Some other time," Tom said. He'd cut down that hornets' nest soon as there was a killing frost, and then he'd show them.

"It's gittin' kind of late anyhow," Lonny said, glancing over his shoulder.

"Yeah, let's just stop by the store an' tell folks about Eddie's still," Harry agreed.

"I gotta get on home," Tom said. The only one he wanted to tell was Pa. And he was going to tell him the whole story, even though Pa might be angry that he'd gone to Eddie's place.

When Tom burst into the cabin, Pa was raking hot coals onto the hearth to set the skillet on. "Where you been, boy? It's 'most supper time," he said irritably.

"You see, after school I was walkin' with Lonny an' Harry, an' we saw Eddie Jarvis go ridin' off toward Ox Gore Holler, lickety-split, an' we—"

"If this is gonna turn into a tale, you'd best set down an' tell it while I fry us these taters an onions," Pa interrupted.

"It's gonna be a tale, all right," Tom said, sitting down on one of the stools in front of the fireplace.

By the time Tom had finished his story, Pa was scraping the potatoes and onions onto their plates. "Wal," he said, pulling his chair up to the table, "ain't nobody gonna miss Eddie. He couldn't talk for cussin', an' he was mean as a ol' hog." He blew on his coffee to cool it. "Yessir, a lot of folks are gonna be thankin' me, once word of this gits 'round."

"How'd you know Eddie was double-crossin' Big Jim, anyhow?"

"He wasn't. He wouldn't of dared."

Shocked, Tom stared across the table. He could hardly believe what he'd just heard. Everybody knew June Higgins never lied.

Pa leaned across the table and demanded, "Did you tell Ol' Man Barnes exactly what I told you to?"

Tom nodded. "I said, 'Tell Mary to let her boyfriend know that Eddie Jarvis might be—' " *Might be.* That was why Pa had insisted that he memorize the message word for word.

"You know I don't lie, boy," Pa said. "Eddie *might* of been double-crossin' that bootlegger, an' I *did* set Big Jim on him. You seen that for yourself."

"If Eddie'd been home, I think that bootlegger would of killed him," Tom said slowly, remembering the man's cold smile.

Pa shook his head. "Nah. He'd of threatened him, an' maybe roughed him up a bit, but Big Jim wouldn't of killed off one of his biggest suppliers. 'Course, Ol' Man Barnes might of led Eddie to think Big Jim was gonna kill him," Pa added, looking wise.

He should have known Pa wouldn't have put Eddie in danger of his life, Tom realized, a little ashamed of the feeling of relief that flowed over him. But as he remembered the gleam of Big Jim's gold tooth, Tom wished the bootlegger had never found his way to the little settlement at Nathan's Mill—and even beyond.

The next day was Saturday, and Tom helped Pa cut and split logs to fill the Widow Brown's woodshed. By late morning, Tom was exhausted, but when he stopped to rest, Pa shook his head and said, "Settin' in that schoolhouse all day long's makin' you soft, boy."

"I ain't soft," Tom protested. He picked up his ax again and began to swing it in rhythmic arcs, splitting the logs he and Pa had cut into stove lengths with the two-man saw. When he heard a holler, Tom was glad for the excuse to stop for a moment. "That's Lonny," he said. "But what's all the racket?"

To Tom's amazement, Lonny and Harry lurched into sight on Eddie Jarvis's wagon. Brambles hung from its sides, vines dangled from the spokes of the wheels, and its heavy load of cornmeal sacks had slid forward. "We heard a ax over this way an' figured it might be you," Lonny called, brushing some twigs off his shoulder.

Mrs. Brown came out on her porch and asked, "What you boys got there? An how on earth did you git that ol' wagon down my path?"

The boys greeted her respectfully, and Lonny explained, "We're takin' Eddie's cornmeal to the mission for Miz Taylor. She's plannin' on keepin' it to give out to folks who fall on hard times."

"We was tryin' to park the wagon a ways off the road when this ol' mule took a notion to come down the path. Would of knocked our heads off on a low branch, if we hadn't of ducked." Harry sounded disgusted.

"How come you two are helpin' Miz Taylor?" Tom asked, feeling a little jealous.

"She an' the preacher was at Eddie's place when we stopped by to have another look 'round. The preacher's busy bustin' up Eddie's still, so Miz Taylor put us to work loadin' the wagon an' asked us to drive it home for her," Lonny explained. "We gotta take them sacks of sugar to the store so she can sell 'em back to Ol' Man Barnes, too."

Pa said, "Wal, don't let us hold you up," and taking the hint, the boys waved good-bye to Mrs. Brown. After some more difficulty with Eddie's mule, they managed to get the wagon turned around, scraping the gatepost in the process.

"I'm surprised that cornmeal an' sugar didn't disappear before Miz Taylor had a chance to move it out," Tom said. "An' Eddie's big ol' still pot, too."

"Folks probably didn't dare take nothin' for fear Eddie might be comin' back."

Alarm for Mrs. Taylor spread through Tom. "You think he will?" he asked urgently, his voice rising.

"Use your head, boy. 'Course he won't. He'd of left that dog of his to guard the place if he was. Now stop worryin' about your teacher an' git back to work, you hear?"

"I hear," Tom said automatically. He was glad Eddie Jarvis finally had to pay for sending the revenuers to look for Pa's still, and he was relieved that Pa had handled it the way he did. No wonder folks looked up to a man who could settle a score like that without bloodshed. Being driven from the hills where he'd lived his whole life was a hard punishment, but it was better than Eddie deserved, Tom thought as he picked up the ax again.

25

Lonny Rigsby was leaning against a tree at the edge of the clearing when Tom left the schoolhouse one Friday in mid-October. "You an' your pa comin' to our corn shuckin' tonight?" Lonny asked as Tom walked toward him.

"Wouldn't miss it!" Tom said.

Lonny lowered his voice and said, "Doc Mowbray was tellin' folks down at the mill how he an' Sol are gonna bring their own red ears."

Tom frowned. Corn shuckings were supposed to be good family fun, with storytelling while everybody stripped the shucks off the corn and a drink of whiskey—or, in this case, Pa's apple brandy—as a prize when somebody pulled the shuck off an ear with red kernels. But if Doc and his brother brought a supply of red ears with them, they'd soon be knee-walking drunk.

"I'm glad your pa's gonna be there. Everybody knows King Higgins is the only one that can keep them Mowbrays in line," Lonny said, falling into step beside Tom. "You read the Bible through yet?" he asked suddenly.

"Ain't started it," Tom said, deciding not to mention that he was halfway through the book Amy had given him.

"Thought maybe you'd be readin' it so's you'd have somethin' to talk about with your girlfriend. She's back for a visit 'cause she got so homesick at that boardin' school they sent her off to."

Amy was back! That must be why Mrs. Taylor had

seemed so cheerful today. Hoping his face didn't show the pleasure he felt at that news, Tom said, "She don't talk about the Bible. She just talks about the evils of drink."

"Speak of the devil," Lonny muttered, and Tom saw Amy coming toward them on Agamemnon. She didn't look like she'd changed a bit, but then she'd only been gone a month.

Grinning from ear to ear, Lonny said, "See you at the corn shuckin', lover boy," and leaving Tom standing by the footlog, he continued along the wagon road toward the settlement.

Amy dismounted and stood beside Tom. "What's a corn shucking?" she asked, just as if she'd never been away, and just as if Tom hadn't walked off without saying good-bye the day before she left.

"It's when everybody meets in a neighbor's barn in the fall to help him pull the shucks off his corn," Tom said, rubbing Agamemnon's nose. "Folks been looking forward to the Rigsbys' shuckin' for weeks now."

Amy frowned and asked, "Why? It doesn't sound like any fun at all."

"It's the storytellin' that's fun," Tom said. "An' the visitin', an' the chance to have some square dancin' when the work's done."

"But how can you stand the smell?"

It took Tom a moment to figure out what Amy was talking about. "The animals are still outside this time of year except in bad weather, an' besides, you ain't down where their stalls are," he explained. "You're up top where they store the feed. The Rigsbys have a two-story barn built into a hillside, see, an' in the back, they can walk right into where they keep their animals, an' out front they can walk—or even drive their wagon—right into the top floor."

Amy waved to a group of little girls walking home from school, but the children looked from Amy to Tom and then ran past them, giggling.

Tom felt his face getting hot, but Amy said, "Don't mind them. They don't understand that a boy and a girl can be plain ordinary friends instead of boyfriend and girlfriend." Then she added matter-of-factly, "I really missed you when I was away at school, Tom. You and my parents. And Princess and Agamemnon, of course. I don't know what I'd have done if Mother hadn't arranged with the school for me to come home for a few days. Or if she hadn't had money for my ticket to Buckton."

"Your ma has her own money?" The words slipped out before Tom could stop them.

Nodding, Amy said, "She says a woman must always have some money of her own so she and her children don't have to be victims of her husband's hardheadedness."

Tom was embarrassed that Amy would tell him something that private, but then he realized she knew he'd never repeat it. Not sure what he should say, he muttered, "I gotta go now," and hurried across the footlog. He thought about Amy as he climbed the mountain. He was glad to know he could have her for a friend instead of a girlfriend, but he didn't think he'd try to explain that to anyone else. Except maybe the Widow Brown.

By the time Tom and Pa walked into the Rigsbys' barn that evening, almost everyone else was already there. Glancing around, Tom saw ears of corn piled high in the middle of the floor and the neighbors sitting on benches arranged along the walls. To his relief, the Mowbray brothers were nowhere to be seen.

Tom headed for the bench where Harry and Lonny had saved space for him and Pa. Across the barn, Andy was busily writing in his notebook, but he looked up and frowned when a loud voice called from the door, "Let's git this floor cleared off so we can dance!" Tom's heart fell when he saw Doc Mowbray, and Sol right behind him.

Doc and Sol picked their way through the crowded barn to where one of their cousins had made room for them on a bench by pushing three of his children onto the floor. Tom saw Lance Rigsby and Pa exchange a long look. It was a good thing Pa was here, he thought uneasily.

"We can't work without no story," Hube Baker called.

"Wal," said Lance Rigsby, "we got some of the best storytellers in Virginia here to entertain us tonight, so . . ." His voice died away when he saw Preacher Taylor and Amy standing in the doorway. There was a strained silence in the barn until Lance recovered and said with false heartiness, "Come in, come in. Glad to have you here. Come on in an' find a seat."

Pa cleared his throat and said, "There's room for you on this bench here if a couple of these young'ns don't mind movin'."

Tom nudged Harry and Lonny, and the three of them slipped off the bench to sit cross-legged on the floor. All eyes followed the preacher and Amy as they made their way across the barn, and Tom wondered why Preacher Taylor had wanted to come, after his experience at the bean stringing.

"Hey, Lance!" Doc Mowbray called, pulling something out of his overalls pocket. "I'm the first one to find a red ear!"

Lance Rigsby glanced toward the preacher and saw that he was talking to Pa, unaware of what was going on. Quickly, Lance passed the jar to Doc and moved so that he blocked the preacher's view of the man lifting it to his lips. Rubbing his hands together nervously, Lance said, "Miz Brown, will you tell us your tale now?"

The Widow Brown said, "I don't have no tale for tonight"—she held up a hand to quell the groaning—"but I can tell you about somethin' that happened just last week over in Ox Gore Holler. . . ."

Soon Tom had forgotten about the Mowbray brothers. The lantern light cast ghostly shadows on the walls, and the only sounds in the Rigsbys' barn were the rasp of the shucks being ripped from the ears of corn and the Widow Brown's voice. ". . . An' next time you go to Ox Gore Holler," the old woman said, bringing her story to a close, "mark my words, you'll see white butterflies flutterin' all 'round the tree where that beautiful girl in the long white dress hanged herself 'cause of her faithless lover."

People stomped and hollered in appreciation, and when the noise began to die down, Lance Rigsby said, "How about it, Jonah? You got a tale for us tonight?"

But before Jonah Simpson could reply, Doc Mowbray held up a red ear of corn and said, "Hey, everybody— lookee what I found! Somebody pass me that jar so I can have my drink."

Doc's brother Sol pulled a red ear out of his pocket and said, "Save some for me, Doc!"

There was a mixture of laughter and grumbling as each

man drank a long pull from the jar, and Tom heard the preacher ask Pa, "Why can't I convince you people that liquor's evil?"

"The likker folks 'round here are makin' nowadays is evil, all right," Pa said.

"You know that's not what I mean, Higgins. *All* liquor's evil."

"Wal, you don't have to worry none tonight, preacher, 'cause that's apple brandy in Cat's jar."

Tom grinned as he listened to the conversation behind him, but he was beginning to feel uneasy. Brandy was even stronger than corn whiskey, and the Mowbray brothers weren't just sipping it. They were a sorry lot when they were sober, but when they were drunk . . .

"I can't sit here with people drinking right in front of me and not speak out," the preacher said. He started to stand up, but Pa pulled him back.

"You're a guest here, Preacher. You can't embarrass your host like that," Pa said sternly.

Silently, Tom thanked him. Everyone was welcome at a corn shucking, but folks wouldn't take it well if the preacher caused a commotion and ruined their good time.

When the clamor died down, Jonah said, "I'm gonna tell you all a story I heard from my wife's mother's brother."

"Tell it, Jonah," called Sol, "but pass me that jar again first. I've found me another red ear."

"How many of them has he got in his pocket there?" grumbled Cat Johnson. Then in a louder voice he said, "Better make sure you save back some of that brandy in case one of us really does shuck a red ear, Lance."

There was a murmur of agreement, and Lance Rigsby

said, "Nothin' to worry about there, Cat. Nothin' to worry about." He glanced imploringly at Jonah Simpson.

Jonah cleared his throat and said, "A while ago, there was a feller named Jack, an'—"

"Whoopee! Pass me that jar again!" hollered Doc Mowbray, holding up another red ear.

"And then pass it over here to me," Cat Johnson said.

Tom felt a little sorry for Jonah Simpson. Nobody would dare interrupt Pa's story that way.

"Let's see your red ear, Cat," Hube Baker called from the other side of the slowly diminishing pile of corn.

Tom was surprised when Cat Johnson held up an ordinary ear of yellow corn.

"That ain't no red ear," several men called out.

"Maybe not, but it's a ear I shucked fair and square, right here in this barn tonight," Cat retorted.

Ol' Man Barnes said, "Pass him the jar. He's got as much right to a drink as Doc an' Sol," and several other men echoed his words.

Sol got unsteadily to his feet and challenged, "You sayin' I didn't shuck this here red ear?"

"Nobody's sayin' you didn't shuck this here red ear, Sol. I'm just sayin' you didn't shuck this red ear *here*," Cat answered.

Sol glowered as all around him men slapped their knees and roared with laughter. Behind him, Tom heard Pa say quietly, "He's drunk. You'd better take your li'l gal on home, Preacher. We're gonna have trouble here tonight."

"But as the spiritual leader of these people, it's my duty to—"

"You ain't no kind of leader if folks don't foller you," Pa interrupted roughly. "Now git!"

But it was too late. A woman screamed, and children

scrambled out of the way as Sol and Cat met near the front of the barn and began circling in a half crouch. Their shadows danced on the barn's walls, huge and menacing.

"Somebody stop them!" Amy cried.

"Quiet, girl," Pa growled.

Tom held his breath and watched. Sol Mowbray was a dirty fighter. Even drunk, he wouldn't have taken on a man as strong as Cat Johnson unless— Tom saw the lantern light reflect off something in Sol's hand at the same instant that Cat's small son shouted, "Look out, Pa! He's got him a knife!"

A split second later, Cat's own knife flashed in the flickering light. Tom's eyes fastened on its blade as Cat held it waist high, ready to thrust it upward. Warily, the two men circled, feinting and parrying. Sol lunged at Cat, but Cat deftly stepped aside, pivoting on his heel to face Sol again. Tom's mouth was dry, and he felt his stomach knot up. Then he sensed a movement behind him as Pa rose to his feet.

"Enough of this!" Pa bellowed. "Put away them weapons, both of you, an' set back down so Jonah can tell his story." The men stopped their circling, but neither took his eyes off the other, and each held his weapon ready.

"At the count of three, I want them knives closed," Pa said.

Except for the wailing of a small child, the barn was silent, and all eyes were fastened on the two armed men. Tom held his breath as Pa began to count. "One . . . two . . . three!"

To Tom's immense relief, Cat took a step backward and snapped his knife closed, and Sol fumbled until his weapon, too, was closed.

"Now go on back to your places," Pa said.

The tension broken, Tom's shoulders slumped, and everyone began to talk at once as Sol and Cat backed away from each other and made their way toward their seats.

But Doc Mowbray, his flushed face twisted with anger, stood up and shook his fist at Sol. "You ain't no Mowbray, walkin' away from a fight like that! Go on back an' finish what you started!" Sol hesitated, looking from his brother to Pa, and Doc gave his brother a mighty shove, crying, "Go on, I tell you!"

Caught off balance, Sol staggered backward and smashed into one of the wooden posts supporting the barn roof. Women screamed and men shouted warnings when the lantern that had been hanging from a nail in the post fell and broke. Kerosene splashed in all directions as the lantern base rolled erratically across the floor. In an instant, flames ignited the litter of corn shucks, and fingers of fire reached toward the straw. Mothers snatched up small children, and men pushed their wives toward the door ahead of them.

A confusion of shapes surged through the clouds of dark smoke, and Tom felt himself propelled forward. He struggled to keep his footing as he was carried along by the panic-stricken crowd. The heat and crackle of the fire were terrifying, and its acrid smoke choked Tom and made his eyes burn. And then he stumbled through the barn door and gasped in huge gulps of fresh night air. Someone hurried him farther away from the barn and then was gone. Pa was safe, he realized thankfully.

From the fringes of a silent group of men, Tom watched the flames lick their way up toward the roof. And then, silhouetted against the glare of the fire, Preacher Taylor staggered from the barn carrying a small, still form.

Tom stood as if paralyzed while the men ran forward. One of them—it was Lance Rigsby—took the preacher's burden and, carrying it gently, hurried toward the house while the others led the gasping preacher away from the burning building. Tom's eyes followed Lance and saw the women who had gathered on the porch scatter to let him pass and then close ranks again to follow him inside.

Tom ran to the house on trembling legs, but when he tore open the door, Mrs. Rigsby blocked his way. "You can't come in here, Tom," she said. "I'm sorry—I know how you feel about Miz Brown."

Tom sank down onto the porch steps and rested his head in his hands. It *was* Mrs. Brown. He'd known all along it was. How could this have happened? And how could it have happened so fast? He sat huddled against the wall, scarcely aware of the door opening and closing or of people passing him as they went in and out. But he roused hinself when he felt a touch on his shoulder, and he looked up into the preacher's drawn, smoke-stained face and red-rimmed eyes. Tom hauled himself to his feet, but he couldn't bring himself to speak, and for once the preacher seemed to have nothing to say. When Pa gave a shout, they both turned toward the sound.

"I think everybody's accounted for except Sol Mowbray an' Miz Brown," he said as he hurried toward them.

"Sol! He may be lying in there, unconscious!" cried Preacher Taylor, starting for the burning barn.

"Don't be a fool!" Pa shouted, jerking him back. And as the preacher struggled against Pa's grip, the fire ate through the barn's center beam and the roof collapsed with a *whumph*, sending sparks high into the air. While the crowd watched, hypnotized, the flames leaped like a living creature and then fell back as the walls crumpled inward.

A slurred voice broke the awed silence that followed, saying, "Ain't that a sight, folks? Ain't that a sight?"

"Wal," Pa said, releasing the preacher from his grasp, "Now we know Sol Mowbray's safe, but I sure am worried about Miz Brown."

"She's inside," the preacher said stiffly, straightening his jacket. "The women are looking after her, but I don't see how she can last the night."

But she was still alive! Tom felt a rush of hope.

Lantern light spilled from the door as Andy stepped onto the porch. "I thought she'd gotten out," he said haltingly when he saw them. "I thought she was safe."

26

Early the next morning, the neighbors gathered at the Rigsbys' to wait for news of the Widow Brown, and for once Tom and Pa were among the first to arrive. The women sat in the house, but the men stayed outside. They stood in small groups, hands deep in their pockets, shoulders hunched against the damp cold. Now and then, two or three of them would disappear into the woodshed for a few minutes—probably for a swallow of apple brandy, Tom thought numbly.

His heart beat faster when the door of the house opened and the doctor appeared on the porch, followed by some of the women. "He's been in there most of the night," Lonny said at Tom's elbow.

The men had moved closer to the house and waited silently for the doctor to speak. "I've done all I can," he said wearily. "She's resting quietly, but I can't say whether she'll recover. It's out of my hands now."

Resting quietly? In his whole life, Tom had never seen Mrs. Brown rest.

Harry nudged Tom and said, "Here comes your girlfriend."

That Harry never did know what was fitting, Tom thought. He ignored Harry's comment and asked Lonny, "You think the Mowbrays are comin'?"

"Pa said he don't know which would be worse, if they come or if they stay away," Lonny said.

"Fact is," Harry said, "I'm kinda surprised your pa's here today, Tom."

"Why wouldn't he be? Miz Brown is a good friend of ours."

"But if your pa had kept them Mowbrays under control like he should of, there wouldn't of been no fire, an' Miz Brown wouldn't be lyin' in there now."

Tom was stunned. How dare Harry! "You'd best be careful what you say," Tom cried, giving him a shove.

But before the other boy could retaliate, a voice said, " 'A soft answer turneth away wrath but grievous words stir up anger.' Haven't we had enough violence around here?" Tom turned and saw the preacher looking at him with disapproval.

"You should show some respect," Amy added, "with Mrs. Brown dying not fifty feet away."

Tom was speechless, stung by her words.

Mrs. Taylor turned to her daughter and said evenly, "Tell the younger children some stories to keep them quiet, Amy." Then she rested a hand on her husband's arm and said, "I'll deal with these boys, Charles."

Looking chastened, Amy started toward the group of children swinging on a knotted rope hung from a tree limb. But the preacher hesitated until Mrs. Taylor pointed toward the woodshed, where Andy stood alone. "Andy looks as if he could use some words of consolation," she said.

Lonny and Harry slipped away, but Mrs. Taylor didn't seem to care. She looked at Tom, a concerned expression on her face. "You usually use your wits instead of your fists, Tom. Harry must have said something terrible to provoke you just then."

"He blamed Pa for what happened to Miz Brown," Tom said, almost choking on the words. He hadn't meant to tell her, but something about the way she looked at him seemed to pull the truth out.

"You mean because Doc and Sol Mowbray had been drinking your pa's brandy?"

Tom shook his head. "Because if Pa had kept Doc and Sol under control, there wouldn't of been no fire an' then Miz Brown—" He stopped as his eyes filled with tears.

"You might as well blame everything on Lance Rigsby because he invited people to the corn shucking," Mrs. Taylor said, her voice tinged with impatience. "The fire was an accident, and it's no one's fault that Mrs. Brown was overcome by the smoke. Nothing anybody says—not Harry Perkins, not even Mr. Taylor—can change that fact. Look at me, Tom. Do you understand what I'm saying?"

Tom forced himself to meet her eyes. "I think so, ma'am."

"Just remember," she said earnestly, "you mustn't ever let anyone make you blame your pa for what happened. Not anyone."

Puzzled, Tom watched her walk toward the house. What had she been trying to tell him? He ran his mind back over her words, searching for her meaning, and all at once his stomach lurched and he had to swallow hard to keep his breakfast down. She knew it was Pa's apple brandy Sol and Doc had been drinking! And she'd as much as told him her husband was going to blame what had happened on the brandy and on the man who'd made it. What if folks believed him? What if they blamed Pa instead of the Mowbrays for what had happened to Mrs. Brown?

Tom squeezed his eyes shut, trying unsuccessfully to blot out the image of last night's terrible events. A commotion in front of the woodshed distracted him, and he blinked when he saw Preacher Taylor, a jar in each hand, pouring Lance Rigsby's apple brandy out into the dirt. The men—even Pa—just stood there and watched him do it.

" 'Who hath woe?' " the preacher called out in the ringing voice he used in the pulpit. " 'Who hath sorrow? Who hath contentions? Who hath babbling? Who hath wounds without cause?' " He paused meaningfully and looked at each of the men standing uncertainly before him. Then he raised his gaze to the women listening from the porch and asked, " 'Who hath redness of eyes?' " Looking back at the men again, he provided the answer: " 'They that tarry long at the wine; they that go and seek mixed wine.' "

Tossing the empty jars into a clump of dead grass,

Preacher Taylor said, "Those words of scripture could have been written for the people of Bad Camp Hollow and Nathan's Mill, because we are all gathered here, woeful and sorrowing. . . ."

Why, he said "we," Tom thought with surprise. And then to his even greater surprise, he noticed that the men were listening respectfully, and that some of the women had come closer so that they could hear better.

Preacher Taylor drew his impromptu sermon to a close, saying, "The doctor has done all that is humanly possible for Mrs. Brown. She is in God's hands. Let us bow our heads and ask that she may once again walk among those who love her."

After the prayer was finished and the quiet echoes of heartfelt "Amens" had faded away, Tom whispered to Pa, "How come Lance let Preacher Taylor pour out all his apple brandy? An' how come everybody listened to him talkin' that way?"

"Don't you think goin' back in that burnin' barn for Miz Brown—an' tryin' to go back again lookin' for Sol—earned that man the right to do an' say pretty much whatever he pleases 'round here?" Pa asked gruffly.

Slowly beginning to understand, Tom said, "I think it made him think 'we' instead of 'you people,' too. You gonna check your Bible an' make sure he wasn't just pretendin' it said all that about woe an' sorrow from drinkin'?"

"Nope. It said that, all right."

"How come you're so sure?"

Pa looked down at him and said, " 'Cause if he'd made it up, he'd of said apple brandy instead of wine."

"I guess he would of," Tom agreed. "You think he knows we made that brandy?"

"Nah. If he knew, he wouldn't of been able to keep quiet about it this long."

Tom decided Pa was right. The preacher wasn't one to bide his time. And that meant Mrs. Taylor hadn't told him she'd found out—or figured out—Pa was making fruit brandy now.

"I can't believe there's going to be a picnic at a time like this," Amy said, suddenly appearing beside Tom. She gestured toward Lonny's brothers, who were laying wide boards across sawhorses to make tables.

"The women bring food to 'most any kind of gathering—hog-killin' time, a marriage, funerals, too," Tom said. "One day soon we'll have a barn raisin' for the Rigsbys, an' the women will bring food here again." His eyes turned toward the charred rubble where the barn had stood.

"Look at all they're bringing out," Amy said, interrupting his thoughts. "I'd better go help."

Hoping the rain that had been threatening all day would hold off awhile longer, Tom wandered over to join Lonny and Harry. Their earlier scuffle forgotten, the three boys waited impatiently until all the grown-ups had filled their plates. When it was finally their turn to go up to the long table, Tom's eyes fell on a dish of cucumber pickles like the ones the Widow Brown always made. With a pang, he thought of the old woman "resting quietly" instead of bustling around and making sure the bowls and platters of food were refilled. And then the preacher walked by, talking earnestly to Andy, and Tom caught the words "whole tragic series of events would never have been set in motion if that jar of moonshine hadn't—"

"Ain't you gonna eat?" Harry asked as he loaded his plate with fried chicken.

Tom shook his head. "I don't feel so good. Tell Pa I've gone on home," he said, setting down his empty plate.

Walking slowly up the mountain, eyes downcast, Tom tried to sort things out. Who was he to believe, Mrs. Taylor or the preacher? Mrs. Taylor was right that the fire was an accident, but the preacher was right when he said the accident was "set in motion" by men who were drunk. And there was no getting around the fact that the Mowbray brothers were drunk from Pa's apple brandy.

Did that mean what happened was Pa's fault? And maybe his fault, too, since he'd helped Pa make the brandy? *Would it be his fault if Mrs. Brown died?*

In an anguished voice, Tom cried out, "If she gits well, I'll never make moonshine—any kind of moonshine—again as long as I live!"

27

When church was over the next morning, little clumps of neighbors stood some distance from the building, talking quietly and shaking their heads. Before the service, as news spread that the Widow Brown seemed to be recovering, the mood of the crowd had been almost festive. But now the atmosphere was sullen.

Tom stood listening to the men talk, hoping the preacher's sermon against moonshine hadn't made them blame Pa for the fire.

"If Preacher Taylor thinks I'm gonna stop passin' 'round a jar of drink 'cause of what happened Friday night, he's got another think comin'," Lance Rigsby declared. "He just don't understand hospitality."

Heads nodded in agreement, and Harry's father added, "An' he don't understand that if folks stayed away from wherever a jar of moonshine was gonna be passed 'round, they wouldn't never go no place at all."

"I don't think nobody's gonna stop stillin' just 'cause the preacher blamed that fire on moonshine," a man from Ox Gore Hollow said belligerently. "I sure ain't."

Tom felt weak with relief. The preacher might have earned the right to say whatever he pleased, but that didn't mean folks had to agree with it, he thought.

Pa turned to leave. "I gotta arrange with Cat Johnson to git some of his late apples for our last run of brandy," he said.

"*Your* last run of brandy," Tom muttered, following Pa with his eyes.

"Who you think you're talkin' to?"

Tom turned and saw Lonny and Harry grinning at him. "Myself, I guess," he admitted.

"Looks like you can talk to your girlfriend now, instead," Lonny said as Amy walked past. "Hey, Amy," he called. "I didn't know you approved of drinkin' likker." Obviously enjoying her shocked reaction, he added, "An' don't tell me you don't, 'cause I saw you there at our corn shuckin', an' your pa said just now that bein' where folks was drinkin' was the same as sayin' you approved."

Amy's eyes flashed with anger. "I didn't know there'd be liquor! Tom never told me that."

"You an' your pa never left when Doc an' Sol started

drinkin'," Lonny said, giving Tom a look that clearly held him responsible for Amy and the preacher being at the corn shucking.

"Your pa didn't say nothin', neither. Guess he only feels safe enough to object when he's up there in his pulpit," added Harry.

Tears of rage filled Amy's eyes. "How dare you—" she began, her voice shaking.

"Preacher Taylor was gonna say somethin', but Pa told him since he was a guest he'd better keep still," Tom said, coming to her rescue.

Deflated, the two boys wandered off, and Amy turned to Tom. "Thanks, Tom," she said. Lowering her voice, she added, "I'm almost glad I have to leave tomorrow. Being homesick wasn't nearly as bad as being home."

Tom glanced quickly around to make sure no one was listening, and then he whispered, "I gotta tell you somethin' before you go, Amy. Remember that day you asked me what I was gonna be when I grew up an' I said—"

"I remember what you said," Amy interrupted.

"I've changed my mind."

"Tom! That's wonderful news!"

Heads turned toward them and Tom quickly said, "I don't mean it to be news. It's still kind of a secret."

A look of understanding came over Amy's face and her eyes strayed to Pa. "I won't tell anyone but my parents," she promised. "It's all right if I tell them, isn't it?"

"You can tell your ma," Tom said reluctantly, "but I ain't ready for nobody else to know yet." He didn't want the preacher thinking it was that sorry sermon that had changed his mind about being a moonshiner. He didn't want the preacher to know before Pa did, either, and he still hadn't figured out how to tell Pa.

* * *

Tom wasn't surprised when Mrs. Taylor asked him to stay after school the next day. "Amy told me you've decided not to be a moonshiner," she said, beaming the smile that always made him melt inside. "I was so glad to hear that! And I know your mother would be proud of your decision if she were alive."

Tom's heart fell. It was one thing to mislead Amy—or the preacher—and quite another not to be honest with Mrs. Taylor. "Ma *is* alive," he said reluctantly. " 'Least I think she is. When I said she'd been gone six years, Amy thought I meant she'd died. But she didn't die. She left."

Mrs. Taylor's eyes widened in surprise. "*Left?* Your mother *left* you?"

Miserable, Tom nodded. "Took my little sisters an' went off, leavin' me for Pa to raise up."

"The poor, poor woman," Mrs. Taylor whispered, as if to herself. "How very desperate she must have been!"

The poor, poor woman? That wasn't the reaction Tom had braced himself for! He'd never thought about how his mother might have felt when she left him and Pa. Tom stole a look at Mrs. Taylor. She was staring out the window, and he wondered if she'd ever been tempted to take Amy and leave the preacher.

Quickly putting that idea out of his mind, he said. "Me an' Pa get on fine. 'Least we have till now. But he don't know yet that I ain't gonna help him make moonshine no more." Realizing too late that Mrs. Taylor hadn't known he worked with Pa, Tom explained uncomfortably, "It's pretty hard for just one person to run a still, you see."

Mrs. Taylor gave him a searching look and said, "The thing that puzzles me is how an honest man like your pa can justify running a still after he promised the judge he'd stop.''

"He never promised he'd stop stillin', ma'am. He just promised he wouldn't make corn likker no more.''

A look of understanding crossed Mrs. Taylor's face. "And now you're worried about what will happen when he finds out you're not going to help him any longer."

Tom nodded. "He'll be plenty mad, all right. Guess he'll have to hire out at apple-pickin' time to get money to pay his land taxes. He don't trust nobody else to work with him, you see.'' Nobody else but Andy, that is, he added silently. And once Andy had written his chapter on moonshine, he'd want to be off collecting more songs and stories instead of helping Pa.

"It's a pity there's not something your pa could do all year,'' Mrs. Taylor mused. "A man like him needs to keep busy.''

Tom wondered how she knew that. It was something he'd never thought about, but remembering how irritable Pa always was during the winter, he realized it was true.

"Isn't there something else he can do besides make moonshine?'' Mrs. Taylor asked, frowning.

"He can fix 'most anything, an' he can make chairs,'' Tom answered.

"Chairs! I should have thought of that, since I'm sitting on a chair he made.''

Wondering why she seemed so pleased, Tom hesitated a few moments before he asked, "Can I go see Princess now?''

Mrs. Taylor gave a little start and then smiled at him. "I was a million miles away, Tom—or a couple hundred, anyway. Of course you may go, and I should, too,'' she said, standing up. They left the building together, and as they walked toward the mission house, Mrs. Taylor rested her hand on Tom's arm. "I have an idea that might help your pa—and a lot of your neighbors—earn some money and bring other people pleasure at the same time."

As Tom threw a stick for Princess and played tug-of-war with her when she brought it back, he thought about what Mrs. Taylor had said. He couldn't imagine what she was talking about, but somehow he felt a little better, anyway.

That evening after supper, Tom and Pa were sitting in front of the fire when they heard a holler. It was woman's voice, and they looked at each other in surprise for a moment before Tom hurried to the door.

"It's Miz Taylor!" he said. What was she doing here? He ran to open the gate for her.

"Come right in an' set down, Miz Taylor, while Tom here pours you a cup of coffee," Pa called from the porch.

Tom's hand shook a little as he lifted the coffeepot from the hearth. Even though he talked to Mrs. Taylor every day at school, he felt awkward and tongue-tied now.

"Chilly evenin' for a ride," Pa said casually, and Tom realized that he, too, felt a little strange about having Mrs. Taylor as a guest.

"I'm not out for a ride," she said, slipping into a chair. "I came up here to ask you something."

"Wal, I'll answer it for you if I can, ma'am," Pa said, looking surprised.

"Why don't you make chairs instead of moonshine, June?"

Tom caught his breath, but Pa didn't seem to object to

the question. " 'Cause everybody 'round here's already got chairs," he said, "an' chairs don't git used up. Moonshine, now, it gits used up right fast, an' then folks want more."

"That makes sense, June. But couldn't you sell chairs in Buckton?"

"Nowadays, them folks don't want no homemade furniture. They want everything factory made."

Mrs. Taylor leaned toward Pa and said earnestly, "June, there are people who would pay good money for chairs like yours. People who want things made by craftsmen instead of turned out by machines."

"Wal, ma'am," Pa drawled. "when you find them people, you let me know, an' I'll make 'em all the chairs they'll buy."

Tom saw Mrs. Taylor's eyes light up. "Is that a promise, June?"

"That's a promise," Pa said, "but I ain't gonna worry none about havin' to keep it."

Better not be too sure of that, Tom thought.

"I should be on my way," Mrs. Taylor said, handing Tom the empty coffee cup. "It's getting late."

"I'll git Ol' Sal an' ride back with you," Tom said.

Mrs. Taylor looked relieved. "It would be wonderful if you'd ride with me to the Rigsbys', Tom. Charles is meeting me there at eight o'clock."

So that was how she got to come up here by herself, Tom thought as he went to whistle for the horse. She must have told the preacher she was going to the Rigsbys' to sit at the Widow Brown's bedside and didn't bother to mention that she was coming up to their place first. "It's

no wonder she an' Pa git along so well," Tom muttered.
"The way the two of 'em have with words, they've got a
whole lot in common."

28

Tom had no idea what an ice-cream social would be like,
but he knew it was something he didn't want to miss. As
he and Pa approached the mission the next Saturday afternoon they heard shouts and laughter, and Tom paused at
the edge of the clearing to see if he could spot Lonny and
Harry.

"You pay your regards to Miz Taylor before you run
off," Pa said sternly, and embarrassed by the reprimand,
Tom followed him through the crowd toward the preacher
and his wife.

After Mrs. Taylor greeted them warmly, she turned to
her husband. "You can fill the freezers now, Charles," she
said. "The young men have chopped one of the blocks of
ice Mr. Barnes brought from town."

Everyone crowded around to watch while the preacher
poured ice chips and rock salt around the inner containers
of the freezers, and Harry asked, "Who's gonna crank
them things, Preacher Taylor?"

"We'll start with a couple of you boys and end up with
the two strongest men," he answered.

Tom saw Mrs. Taylor give her husband a look of sheer

exasperation and knew she realized there would be fights to settle the question of who was the strongest. Tom wished he could tell her not to worry. These fights would be fair contests, not angry brawls. And nobody would be drunk. He was almost disappointed when Pa spoke up.

"Andy and I will crank the whole time," Pa said, rolling up his sleeves, "an' while we do, Andy will tell us a tale."

But before they could begin, there was a great stir as the Rigsbys' wagon drove up and someone called, "They've brought Miz Brown." Tom ran to see for himself.

It was true! While Lance Rigsby lifted the tiny, quilt-wrapped figure from a mattress in the back of the wagon and headed for a sunny spot, Tom raced to the schoolhouse-chapel and brought out the chair Pa had made for Mrs. Taylor.

"You all just settle down now so I can hear Andy's tale," Mrs. Brown scolded as everyone gathered about her. "It takes more 'n a bit of smoke to stop me. Or to keep me inside on a beautiful Indian-summer afternoon," she added, giving Tom a special smile.

At least she sounded like herself, Tom thought. She was still pale, but she seemed stronger than she'd been when he'd visited her two days ago.

When everyone was once again looking expectantly at Andy, he announced, "Today I'm going to tell some stories for the youngsters. The first one's about a little red hen who wanted to make some bread but didn't have any cornmeal. 'Who will help me plant the corn?' she asked. 'Not I,' said the cat. 'Not I,' said the dog . . .' "

By the time Andy came to the end of his last story, he and Pa were cranking the freezers more and more slowly. "And now, who will help June and me eat all this ice cream?" Andy asked.

"I will!" chorused the small children gathered around his feet.

Smiling, Mrs. Taylor spooned the ice cream into dishes, and the older girls passed them around. As the first taste of the creamy sweetness melted on Tom's tongue, he thought enviously of Ol' Man Barnes's granddaughter Mary riding into Buckton to the ice-cream parlor with the bootlegger a couple times a week.

Two hours later, a second batch of ice cream had disappeared and people were starting home. "That was real nice, Miz Taylor," Tom said as he and Pa left.

"I'm glad you enjoyed it," she said. "Everybody's invited back next Saturday evening for a sing, so if you have a musical instrument, be sure to bring it." Then she turned to Pa. "I want to thank you for preventing any trouble over who was the strongest. I hope I can count on you again next week."

As Tom and Pa started home, Tom said, "Miz Taylor's the nicest woman I know. Next to the Widow Brown, of course." How glad he'd been to see her.

"Smart, too—a lot smarter 'n her husband," Pa said. "She knows you catch more flies with honey than vinegar."

Tom wasn't sure what that was supposed to mean, but he knew Mrs. Taylor's social had made everyone forget the preacher's last sermon. And next week there would be a sing. He was wondering what that would be like when Cat Johnson's little boys called for him and Pa to wait.

The Johnsons caught up, and they all walked together, moving to the edge of the narrow road so that the Rigsbys' wagon could go by, and then passing a young couple carrying two small children.

Tom was sorry when it was time to tell the Johnsons good-bye. It seemed that everybody else was in a family, he thought as he followed Pa across the footlog and started up the steep path. "Pa, do you ever wish you was married?" he asked tentatively.

"I *was* married," Pa said. "Still am, I guess, when you come right down to it." He walked in silence for a few steps before he added, "Be sure you pick yourself a mountain girl, and not some flatlander, when the time comes. Then maybe your marriage will stick. Bein' married takes right smart pullin' together, you know."

Tom blinked in amazement. "Ma was a flatlander?"

Pa gave a grunt that Tom took for "yes" and began to walk faster, but Tom refused to take the hint. "How'd the two of you meet, then?" he asked, scrambling to keep up. This was the closest Pa had come to mentioning his ma since the day she left.

"She grew up on one of them big farms just the other side of Buckton," Pa said reluctantly. "I worked there at harvest time the year the revenuers caught your grandpap at our still an' sent him to jail for six months."

Tom had never known anything about that. "So you an' Ma ran off and got married?"

Pa whirled around so quickly that Tom almost bumped into him. "How come you're askin' so many questions, boy?"

" 'Cause I want to know," Tom said, backing up a few steps and trying not to let the expression on Pa's face force him to look away. "How come you don't want to tell me? You ashamed or somethin'?" His heart pounded wildly—he'd never challenged Pa like this before.

Pa glared at him, and something about the set of his

jaw took Tom back to the day they'd walked down to the store and Pa had announced, "Polly's gone, an' she ain't comin' back. That's all any of you need to know, so don't be askin' me—or Tom—no questions."

Tom felt six years old again. "Don't tell me, then," he said in a thin voice, looking away from Pa's fierce gaze. The silence seemed to stretch to the breaking point, and then it was shattered by the scrunch of Pa's boots on the rocky trail. Hands in his pockets and eyes downcast, Tom followed, determined not to cry. He was almost startled when Pa spoke.

"One day late that winter I heard a knockin' at the door, an' there she was, her face all streaked with tears and plumb tuckered. Her pa'd turned her out, and she'd walked all the way up the mountain to find me—stopped at the settlement an' asked somebody where I lived at."

"But why'd her pa turn her out?"

Pa looked back at him impatiently and said, "Why d'you think? 'Cause you was on the way."

Tom's mind reeled. He stumbled along in a daze, struggling to sort out his thoughts. No wonder Ma left, if she was used to living in a house like the ones he'd seen along the road to Buckton. And no wonder Pa didn't think much of flatlanders, if the one he knew best had gone off and left him with a six-year-old to raise up by himself.

"How come Ma didn't take me with her?" Tom asked, finally putting into words the question that had troubled him for half of his life.

" 'Cause she knew if she did, I'd come after her an' take you back."

Tom felt as though a burden had been lifted from his shoulders. Ma hadn't left him behind because she didn't love him enough, and Pa didn't wish she'd taken him with her.

"So how's it feel, knowin' you're half flatlander?" Pa challenged.

"I ain't no flatlander," Tom objected. "I'm mountain born an' mountain bred, an' I'm gonna live in these hills all my days."

Pa gave a grunt of satisfaction and turned to look back at him. "Just like your ol' man, eh?" he said.

"Just like my ol' man," Tom echoed, adding silently, except I ain't gonna be no moonshiner. But how—and when—was he going to tell Pa that?

29

"I want you down at the still soon as you git through school t'morrer afternoon," Pa announced when Tom came home on Thursday.

Tom felt as though a huge hand were squeezing his heart. "What about Andy? I thought he—"

"Workin' at the still's as much a part of your education as goin' to that school, an' you ain't done nothin' for weeks now."

"I can't—" Tom began.

"What do you mean, you can't?" Pa asked roughly. "You be there! Understand?"

His resolve gone, Tom nodded.

"I asked you a question, an' I ain't heard your answer yet, boy." Pa's voice was deadly quiet.

"I understand," Tom said, turning away and stumbling out the door. Patting his pocket to make sure he had his knife and new block of wood, Tom headed up the path. He'd walk up to the ridge, to the rocky outcropping folks called the overlook, and sit there awhile, whittling, until Pa got over his anger.

Tom was breathing hard by the time he reached the overlook and perched on the edge of the shelflike rock. He let his legs dangle while he watched the ravens soaring below him, and then, squinting against the glare of the late-afternoon sun, he counted the mountain ridges stretching into the distance. The blazing gold foliage on the slope across the hollow was blotched by dark clumps of evergreens, but farther away the colors blended into a mottled blue that grew paler on each successive crest until the mountains seemed to fade into the sky.

The remoteness of the view made Tom feel powerless and alone. Pulling out his knife and the wood, he decided to carve a dog like Princess. He'd hoped to lose himself in his work, but his mind was as busy as his fingers. He was determined not to give in again tomorrow when Pa raised his voice—or used that quiet, threatening tone. Tom tried not to think about what would happen when he refused to help at the still.

Finally, in the chill of approaching dusk, Tom put away his knife, straightened his shoulders, and started home. Pa's flashes of anger never lasted long, so he wasn't worried about this evening. He was worried about tomorrow. Tomorrow, when he'd have to face Pa and not back down, when he'd have to keep the promise he'd made to himself.

"What's that you're sewin'?" Tom asked when he stopped by the Widow Brown's cabin on his way to the still the next afternoon.

"Baby quilt," she replied, biting off a thread.

"Who's havin' a young'n?" Tom asked, interested.

Mrs. Brown smoothed the square she was working on and said, "It's for Miz Taylor." When Tom's mouth fell open, the old woman grinned and explained, "She wants it for somebody she knows that sells ol'-timey handmade things." Then, gesturing to a small, cloth-wrapped bundle on the table, she said, "Now take them ham biscuits for your supper an' go along. Your pa won't be happy if you're late gittin' to the still."

That wasn't all Pa wouldn't be happy about, Tom thought glumly as he left the cabin. The farther he walked, the more apprehensive he became. But in spite of the dryness of his mouth and the thudding of his heart, he kept up his pace. Knowing for sure that Pa wouldn't have let Ma take him away with her gave him the courage he needed, Tom realized.

When he finally made his way through a maze of laurel to the small area Pa and Andy had cleared so they could set up the still, Pa grumbled, "Took your time gittin' here." Hauling himself to his feet, he said, "I'll be back in a couple of hours to see how you're gittin' along. You know what to do till then."

He knew what to do, all right, Tom thought as he watched Pa leave. He just wasn't going to do it. Hunkered down in front of the furnace, Tom listened to the sound made by the thin stream of apple brandy as it flowed from the worm, filtered through the hickory coals and flannel lining the funnel, and dripped into the jar. When he noticed a subtle change in the sound, he knew the liquid had just about reached the top.

Almost hypnotized, he watched as the brandy began to trickle out around the funnel and run down the outside of the jar. The wet stain it made on the ground was hardly as big as a dinner plate when Tom realized it had stopped growing. The fire in the furnace had died down and the liquid in the still pot had cooled, so there was no longer any vapor to condense inside the worm and drip out.

Pa expected him to keep the fire in the furnace hot enough to evaporate the alcohol but not so hot it would scorch the apple pomace. He expected him to replace the jars as they filled up, too. Tom's determination wavered, and he glanced at the two long logs. All he'd have to do was push them further into the furnace and stir up the embers so they'd catch fire. And then if he real quick capped that jar and put another in its place and kicked some pine needles over where the brandy had soaked in—

No. He wasn't going to make moonshine ever again. He'd learn some other craft or trade, one that he could do out in the open. One that couldn't possibly lead to harm. Tom swallowed hard and tried to blot out the image of Preacher Taylor stumbling from the burning barn with a small, limp figure in his arms.

"That night ruined stillin' for me," Tom whispered. Until then, he'd never actually seen anybody drunk. He'd *heard* of men being drunk, of course, and heard of the things they did. He'd even seen Emma Baker's bruises. But it wasn't until he saw Sol Mowbray go after Cat Johnson with a knife that it meant anything to him. It was only when he felt himself caught up in the terror of the fire and its aftermath that what he knew about became real.

It wasn't just the promise he'd made to himself, Tom realized. He wasn't risking Pa's fury simply because of a few words no one else had heard—he really didn't want to make moonshine anymore. Tom felt a little better. He ate his ham biscuits and settled down to wait, half dreading the sound of Pa's step and half wishing he'd come and get it over with. Whatever "it" might be.

Darkness fell, and the cold seemed to settle over the silent woods. Tom buttoned the lightweight jacket Pa had bought him at the clothing bureau and wrapped himself in Pa's blanket. It seemed like hours had passed before he heard a twig snap nearby. His muscles tensed, relaxing only a little when he heard a low voice mutter, "Fire's out. Dadburn boy must of fell asleep."

"I ain't been asleep, Pa," Tom said quietly as a dark shape moved into the small clearing.

"Then how come you let the fire go out?" Pa's low voice shook with rage.

" 'Cause I ain't helpin' you make moonshine no more." Tom had trouble making his lips form the words.

"I don't think I heard you right, boy," Pa said in a voice that was deadly quiet.

Tom's heart pounded against his ribs, but he forced himself to repeat, "I ain't helpin' you make moonshine no more." The next thing he knew, Pa was on one knee beside him, jerking him up by the front of his jacket.

"Did that preacher put you up to this?" Pa demanded harshly.

Tom could hardly breathe, but he managed to choke out, "I decided m-myself."

Pa's words came from between clenched teeth. "An' how come you decided that? Decided to go against your own father? Against your birthright?"

"Because of—of what ha-happened at the cornhuskin'. I—" But Tom never had a chance to finish. Cursing, Pa slapped his face with the back of his hand. Tom's head spun, and he tasted the saltiness of blood.

"Now you git up an' light that there fire," Pa demanded, releasing him.

"I ain't gonna do it. I told you I—" Another powerful backhanded slap cut off Tom's words and made his ears ring. He felt himself start to slump sideways.

Grabbing the front of Tom's jacket again, Pa jerked him back up and said, "Light the fire."

Tom's head was throbbing so hard he couldn't shake it, so he forced his bruised lips to form the word "No."

"Light it!" Pa roared. "Light it, I tell you!"

Tom gasped as the blows rained down on him, and with Pa no longer holding his jacket, he felt himself falling . . . falling . . . until he realized that the pummeling had stopped. From the edge of consciousness, Tom heard a strange sound, a kind of sobbing: "What have I done? What have I done to my boy?"

Tom moaned a little as he felt himself being lifted up, and with his ear against Pa's chest, he felt as well as heard Pa's labored breathing. He was dimly aware of low branches tearing at his pants legs as Pa pushed his way through the dense woods, and then, through half-closed eyes, he saw the pale splash of lantern light that shone from the Widow Brown's window.

Tom felt a bed beneath him and heard Mrs. Brown say, "Git some cold water for the poor boy's face." The door slammed, and Tom heard the old woman's voice again.

"We gotta make sure news of this don't get 'round, Andy. We can't have folks losin' respect for June."

Andy's voice was serious. "You're right, of course. He would lose a lot of his authority if people knew about this."

Tom's head still pounded, but now that he was lying still, he didn't feel quite so groggy. Instead, he felt a growing anger toward his father. Pa was sorry now, but what good did that do? What happened at the still was bad enough, but it was over with. Now, though, if folks weren't going to find out what Pa had done to him, he'd have to stay out of sight. He'd miss school. And, he realized with dismay, he'd miss the sing at the mission tomorrow night. Pa would go because Mrs. Taylor was counting on him to prevent trouble, but *he* would have to stay home. It wasn't fair.

Pa came back to the cabin with the bucket of spring water. "Is he gonna be all right, Miz Brown?" he asked plaintively.

At that moment, Tom realized the tables had been turned. Pa was at his mercy now, and he was going to make the most of it.

"I'll see if I can bring him 'round," Mrs. Brown said, and Tom felt the cold shock as she began to sponge his face with a wet cloth. He lay motionless even when water dripped down his neck and he wanted nothing more than to wipe it away. After a few minutes, Mrs. Brown muttered, "I don't rightly know why he ain't stirrin'."

Pa's voice sounded remorseful. "He was scared, but he stood up to me. Even when I hit him, he didn't back down. I should of been proud of him, but instead I hit him again."

Proud of him! Sudden tears mingled with the cold water

from the Widow Brown's cloth. "Pa?" Tom said, blinking rapidly as he tried to sit up. "Pa?"

"I'm right here, boy," Pa said, awkwardly touching Tom's shoulder. "Lay down an' rest yourself."

Tom eased his aching head back onto the pillow. The showdown was over. It had been awful, but it had been worth it. Pa respected him. And now that he had faced Pa's anger at its worst, he'd never have to fear it again.

30

Even with the Widow Brown's poultices, two weeks passed before the bruises on Tom's face were gone. Most of the trees had lost their leaves now, and as Tom and Pa set off for church in the crisp late-autumn sunshine, the bare branches were silhouetted against the brilliance of the cloudless sky.

"The way you're hurryin' down this mountain, I'd say you'll be right glad to see somebody other 'n me and Andy for a change," Pa said.

"Them two weeks seemed so long," Tom said seriously, "I don't see how a man could live through a whole year in jail."

"Wal, we don't have to worry none about that since I ain't makin' moonshine no more."

"Couldn't you figure out some way to work alone like Eddie Jarvis did?" Tom asked.

Pa shook his head and said quietly, "If drinkin' moonshine makes a feller violent, he hadn't ought to drink it, right?" Tom nodded, and Pa went on. "Wal, if *makin'* moonshine makes a feller violent, then he hadn't ought to *make* it."

Tom didn't know what to say. He couldn't even imagine Pa not making moonshine.

"The way I see it," Pa went on, "a child beater's no better 'n a wife beater, an' I don't like bein' on the same level as Hube Baker."

A wave of feeling washed over Tom. He'd thought Pa's silence the last two weeks showed his disappointment that his son would never make the best whiskey and brandy in the hills. But instead Pa must have been brooding about what he'd done. "You ain't nothin' like Hube," Tom said fervently, but Pa made no response.

By the time they reached the mission, people had already gone into the schoolhouse-chapel. Mrs. Taylor stood up to lead the first hymn, and she smiled at Tom when she noticed him sitting in the back beside Pa. Tom knew she'd have ridden up to visit him if Andy hadn't told her he was sick with measles. But even though he'd missed her, he hadn't wanted her to see his bruises—not for Pa's sake, but because he didn't want her feeling sorry for him.

Outside after the service, Mrs. Taylor told Tom how much he'd been missed at school, and he thanked her for the soup she'd made and sent with Andy. Then she looked up at Pa and asked, "June, how long would it take you to make me three chairs?"

"Couple of weeks, I reckon. You want rockin' chairs or settin' chairs like the one I made you for school?"

"Make one rocker and a pair of chairs like mine," Mrs.

Taylor answered. Then she asked Tom, "How many carvings can you have for me in two weeks?"

He thought of the box of birds and animals beside his mattress in the loft and asked, "How many you want?"

"Bring me all your very best ones," she said as she turned to greet Emma Baker.

"I made that doll family to show you, Miz Taylor," Emma said, holding out a basket filled with corn-husk dolls.

"Wonderful!" Mrs. Taylor exclaimed. "Make me all the dolls you have time for, and be sure each one's a little bit different from the others." After the woman walked away, Mrs. Taylor mused, "I should have asked her where she got that basket."

"Probably from one of the Simpson brothers," Tom said. "They all make 'em, but Jonah's are the nicest." Almost before the words were out of his mouth, Mrs. Taylor was heading toward the edge of the clearing, where Jonah Simpson stood talking with Cat Johnson.

"What's that li'l lady up to now?" Pa asked suspiciously.

"She knows a man in the city who sells mountain crafts," Ol' Man Barnes explained, "an' she's gonna send him things folks make. Whenever anybody buys somethin', he'll send back half the money for the one who made it."

"She's fixin' to make me keep that dadburn promise she tricked me into, if you ask me," Pa grumbled as he went off to find Lance Rigsby.

Lonny and Harry had been listening nearby, and Lonny asked, "What's 'crafts,' anyhow?"

Tom didn't know quite how to answer this, but one of

195

the girls from Ox Gore Hollow did. "Crafts are things folks make by hand," she said importantly.

"City folks ain't gonna want nothin' we make," Harry said.

"If Miz Taylor says they're gonna, then they're gonna," the girl answered confidently. "Miz Taylor told Ma folks that can't make nothin' theirselves hanker after handmade things. They don't always use 'em, though—sometimes they just set an' look at 'em."

Harry sneered and mimicked, " 'Miz Taylor. Miz Taylor.' What's she know, anyhow?"

"She knows a lot," Tom said sharply, adding, "You just got your nose out of joint 'cause no city folks are gonna want to buy your pa's barrels, Harry."

"Yeah, Harry, you're just mad 'cause barrels ain't crafts," Lonny said, grinning.

Turning to his cousin, Harry said belligerently, "Carpenterin' ain't crafts, neither, you know."

As he half listened to his friends' argument, Tom's eyes were on the girl. The way she'd spoken right up just now surprised him—it wasn't the way a mountain girl behaved. It was more like what he'd expect from Amy. Suddenly Tom was aware of an expectant silence and he turned to the boys and asked, "You say somethin' to me?"

"I said," Harry repeated, exaggerating his words, "makin' moonshine's no craft, neither."

"You're right about that," Tom said. "Makin' moonshine the traditional way like Pa an' I did, now that's a art."

Harry squinted at him and repeated, "Like you 'did'?"

That Harry never missed a thing, Tom thought. "Yep," he said, "we gave it up." Unwilling to face the volley of questions he knew would come as soon as Harry and Lonny recovered from their shock, Tom added, "You don't need to know why."

Hands in his pockets, he walked away. When he looked back, Harry and Lonny had wandered off, but the girl from Ox Gore Hollow was still watching him.

31

Tom was hurrying down the mountain to buy tobacco for Pa when he rounded a curve in the trail and came face to face with P. D. Hudson and Cory. His heart began to pound, and he had to remind himself that he no longer had anything to fear from revenuers. Tom stepped aside to let the men pass, but Hudson stopped and asked, "Who's your father buying his corn liquor from these days?"

"Don't think none's been made 'round here since Eddie Jarvis left," Tom said innocently.

Hudson made a sound that might have been a laugh, and he and Cory started up the mountain again. Tom watched the two revenuers trudge purposefully along the trail. Maybe they were going after Hube Baker, he thought, and after a moment's hesitation, he followed them.

It was a public path, Tom reasoned, but just the same, he was glad the men didn't look back and see him. Where the path made a hairpin bend, he struck out through the woods, shortcutting toward the Bakers' side yard. He was headed toward some scrubby cedar trees, thinking that they would shield him from view and allow him to watch both the trail and the house, when someone grabbed him from behind. A gloved hand covered his mouth and a voice hissed, "Oh, no, you don't! You're not going to warn him." It was Ralph, the third revenuer. Tom struggled, but Ralph only held him tighter, shoving him to the ground behind the cedars and pinning him down with a knee in his back.

Tom could see nothing, but he heard the crunch of boots on loose rock, and then there was silence as P. D. Hudson and Cory stopped not ten feet away. "It's there on the porch rail, so everything's all set," Hudson said in a low voice. "Let's go."

Pulling Tom to his feet, Ralph stood up to watch, and Tom saw Emma Baker's red apron hanging on the railing of the porch and the revenuers heading for the henhouse. He watched Cory lift the wooden bar that latched the door and follow Hudson inside. Tom was conscious of Ralph's shallow breathing behind him, and he felt the man's grip relax a moment later when Hudson emerged with Hube. The sound of an ax striking wood came from the small building, and Tom could almost see the wave of fermented mash gushing out of the barrel.

Ralph released him, saying, "I'd better not catch you interfering with our enforcement activities again, kid."

Brushing himself off, Tom glared at the revenuer but said nothing. As he turned to leave, Tom glanced toward the house to see if Emma Baker was watching and noticed that the red apron was gone. Hube must have knocked her upside the head once too often, he thought as he cut back through the woods. But Tom couldn't help feeling a grudging admiration for the old man's nerve, setting up his still in a henhouse not fifty feet from the path and having his wife bar the door from the outside when he was working there. No wonder Hube bragged that he just ignored the warning rifle shots nowadays.

Back on the path again, Tom headed toward the settlement, almost running. He'd have to hurry if he wanted to tell the news before it became common knowledge. Outside the store, he barely paused to admire the revenuers' car, and he ignored the handful of little boys sitting on its running board.

"You pass anybody on your way down here?" Ol' Man Barnes asked casually as he handed Tom the tobacco twists Pa had sent him for.

"Only a couple of revenuers goin' after Hube Baker," Tom answered just as casually. Suddenly the center of attention, he told what had happened—except for the part about the red apron. By the time he went outside, carrying Pa's tobacco, the little boys had disappeared, and Lonny and Harry were leaning against the car.

"You waitin' for them revenuers to come back?" Tom asked.

Lonny nodded. "You gonna wait with us?"

"I already know who they're bringin' down, an' besides, I gotta git on home." Tom turned as if to leave, but Lonny grabbed his arm.

"It's weasel-faced ol' Hube Baker, ain't it?" he said eagerly.

Tom nodded. "Here they come with him now."

As the little procession approached the car, a crowd

gathered, watching silently. "Hey, Mr. Baker," Harry called, "at least you're gonna git yourself a automobile ride out of all this."

"But I'll have a long walk home again come court day," Hube replied, summoning up a grin as he looked between Harry and Tom.

The people backed away when Cory started the engine, and everyone stood and watched until the car was out of sight and the dust began to settle.

"Pa's waitin' on me," Tom told Lonny and Harry as he turned to leave. "We're workin on them chairs he's promised Miz Taylor." No one ever referred to her as "the preacher's wife" anymore, Tom realized. She was always "Miz Taylor."

Emma Baker was sweeping the porch when Tom passed her cabin. "Hey, Miz Baker," he called, waving.

She waved back. "Hey, Tom. You see them revenuers takin' Hube off to jail?"

"Yep, but he didn't seem to think he'd be there long."

"He'll be in Atlanta a year an' a day this time," Emma Baker said confidently, coming over to the fence. Noticing Tom's dubious expression, she added. "Miz Taylor said she'd ask the preacher to see to that. She don't cotton to wife beaters no more 'n he does to moonshiners."

So that was how Emma got word to the revenuers, Tom thought as he continued up the mountain. Imagine Emma turning Hube in! Who'd of thought she had it in her?

The rest of the way home, Tom silently rehearsed the way he'd tell his news. When he walked into the cabin, Pa looked up and growled, "What took you so long?"

"First I got caught by a revenuer, an' then I watched Petey Hudson an' Cory raid Hube's still. Here's your tobacco." Tom tossed it to him and sat down on a stool by the hearth. "Now, what you want me to do?" he asked.

"I want you to tell me the story you been practicin' all the way up this mountain," Pa said irritably, "an' I want you to peel them white oak splits for my chair seat while you're tellin' it."

When Tom had finished his account of the raid, Pa said, "Served him right. Emma should of done it years ago."

She couldn't very well have done it before Mrs. Taylor and the preacher came here, Tom thought. He worked a few minutes in silence before he looked up and said, "I'd like to try carvin' somethin' along the back of one of them chairs, Pa. Along there," he added, pointing to the top of the chair back Pa was working on.

"Before you try that fancy stuff, you gotta learn how to choose your wood, an' weave the seats, an' fit tight joints, an' all the rest," Pa said sternly.

By the time he was a man, Tom thought with satisfaction, he'd be making chairs as fine as Pa's. Even finer, because he'd carve them all, each one a little different—unless, of course, they were a matched set.

A shout brought Tom back to the present. He went to the window, hoping it was Andy coming to see how Pa made chairs, but it wasn't. "It's Preacher Taylor," Tom said, going to the door.

"I been expectin' this," Pa muttered, standing up, "an' I'm ready for him."

The preacher grasped Pa's hand and pumped it up and down. "Congratulations, Higgins," he said heartily. "I always knew that with God's help you could do it."

"It's my boy, here, that helps me, Preacher," Pa said, putting a puzzled look on his face, "an' I been makin'

chairs off an' on 'most all my life. 'Course, I ain't never
had a chance to sell none 'til Miz Taylor got her—uh, her
craft co-op goin'," he added, stumbling a little over the
unfamiliar words.

"You know very well my congratulations are for choosing the straight and narrow path," the preacher said, still
smiling. "If I never achieve anything else in my ministry
here, I'll feel I've succeeded," he added proudly, warming
his hands at the fire.

"An' what exactly do you mean by that?" Pa asked.

Tom glanced at Preacher Taylor, but it was obvious the
man hadn't heard the warning note in Pa's voice.

"Because of my influence, Hube Baker's on his way to
jail, and he'll be tried in a county far enough away that
no one there could possibly be one of his customers. And
the king of the mountain moonshiners"—he gave Pa a
little bow—"has given up his evil practice for good."

"You're dead wrong about a couple of things,
Preacher," Pa said curtly. "What I done wasn't evil, an'
you had nothin' to do with my givin' it up. *Nothin' at all!*"

Tom and the preacher both jumped when Pa thundered
his last words, punctuating them by jabbing his index
finger at the preacher.

Preacher Taylor swallowed hard. "But I thought—"

"I don't care what you thought. Ain't no man on this
earth could force me to give up makin' moonshine—no
preacher, no sheriff, no judge. An' there ain't no law could
make me give it up, neither. You understand that?"

The preacher nodded.

"I decided *on my own* to give up moonshinin', an' don't
you forget it." Pa threw his knife down on the curls of
wood that littered the floor around his shaving horse and

stormed out of the cabin, leaving the preacher staring after him. Tom didn't know what else to do, so he picked up the knife and put it on the mantel.

"At least he told the truth when he said no judge could make him give up making moonshine," the preacher said bitterly. "You and I both know he broke his solemn word to the judge in Buckton."

"That ain't so, Preacher Taylor," Tom protested. He held up his hand when the preacher started to interrupt. "He promised he'd never make corn likker again, and he didn't. He made fruit brandy instead."

The preacher stared at Tom for a moment, speechless, and then leaned against the mantel, his shoulders shaking. Tom was aghast. And then he realized the preacher wasn't crying—he was laughing. *Laughing?*

"Well, Tom," the man said when he could speak again, "that should be a lesson to me." When Tom looked at him blankly, he quoted, " 'Pride goeth before destruction, and a haughty spirit before a fall.' "

Tom wished he'd just say what he meant instead of quoting from the Bible.

"You see, Tom," Preacher Taylor explained as he sat down in the rocking chair, "I was so proud of myself, thinking I'd influenced your father to give up his e—to give up moonshining, that I let myself in for a lot of embarrassment."

Tom nodded, understanding now, and the preacher said ruefully, "All my preaching, and all my talking, and all my work to get the sheriff out here and P. D. Hudson on the job, and then I find out your father decided *on his own* to give up moonshining. How did that happen, anyway?"

"You'll have to ask him." Tom didn't think it was the

preacher's business how that had happened, but he wasn't going to say so.

"Have to ask me what?" Pa asked, coming inside with an armload of wood for the fire.

"To ask you why you decided to give up moonshining, June," the preacher said.

Pa set down his load of wood. "You know, Charles, that dadburn Pro'bition ruined stillin' for honest men."

"I don't quite understand," Preacher Taylor said, frowning.

"The moonshine goin' out of this holler nowadays will rot your gut, if it don't kill you first," Pa said. "Before Pro'bition, there was some bad whiskey made 'round here, but it was made honest. It was bad 'cause the men makin' it didn't have no skill. They wasn't raised up in the moonshine tradition, with fathers teachin' sons down through the generations an' takin' pride in their craft."

Pa paused, and Tom stared down at his feet. A feeling of regret crept over him.

"They was usin' sugar an' yeast instead of makin' pure corn whiskey," Pa went on, "an' sometimes scorchin' it a little 'cause they was careless, but it wouldn't of hurt you none to drink it."

The preacher frowned. "But I don't understand how Prohibition made things worse."

Tom looked at him in surprise. The man seemed to be listening—listening and trying to understand. "I'll tell you how, Preacher Taylor," he said. "A bootlegger came in here an' told folks how to make more whiskey faster, an' he told 'em all kinds of stuff to put in it to trick their customers into thinkin' it was better 'n it was."

The preacher ran his fingers through his hair. "I can see how this happened, human nature being what it is, but I still don't understand why it made your father give up making moonshine." He turned to Pa and said, "I'd think the liquor you made would have been in great demand if no one else's was worth drinking, June."

"It was," Pa agreed. "It was. But them other fellers had gave moonshinin' a bad name."

"So you decided to give it up," the preacher said, wonder in his voice.

"I decided to give it up."

Tom frowned. Pa might pride himself on always telling the truth, but saying things so a person got the wrong idea wasn't all that much different from lying. Pa could have just told the preacher his reasons were private. But then, of course, he wouldn't have felt so clever.

"Well, Brother June, I'm glad you've stopped, whatever the reason," Preacher Taylor said, standing up and holding out his hand again.

Pa grasped it without hesitation. "Makin' chairs is a lot easier 'n makin' moonshine, Charles," he said, "but it sure ain't near as excitin'."

"Tell you what," the preacher said, "you find yourself a thicket somewhere to do your work in, and I'll come looking for you."

Tom grinned. "Maybe we could set up inside that ol' brush tabernacle, if it ain't all blowed down by now, Pa. Preacher Taylor never would think to look there."

"You're right, Tom," the preacher said. "I'd never suspect anyone would make chairs so near the mission."

Tom and Pa walked to the gate with the preacher and stood looking after him as he rode away. "You know, Pa," Tom said thoughtfully, "Preacher Taylor ain't near as bad as he used to be."

"He never was bad so much as just plain misplaced,"

Pa said. "It took him a while to learn his way 'round here in the hills."

The hills. Tom raised his eyes to the stark ridge where the bare trees bristled up against the November sky. Then he turned to Pa and said, "Since I ain't gonna be makin' the best whiskey in these hills, I guess I'll just have to make the best chairs."